THE GOSPEL OF JOSEPH

— A NOVEL —

THE GOSPEL OF JOSEPH

— A NOVEL —

Gabriel Meyer

CROSSROAD • NEW YORK

1994

The Crossroad Publishing Company
370 Lexington Avenue, New York, NY 10017

Printed in the United States of America

Library of Congress Cataloging-in-Publication Data

Meyer, Gabriel, 1947–
    The Gospel of Joseph / Gabriel Meyer.
    p. cm.
    ISBN 0-8245-1406-8
    1. Joseph, Saint—Fiction. I. Title.
PS3563.E873G67 1994
813'.54—dc20   94-21481
                                     CIP

For my father,
the man who saw the lightning

Contents

Map of Herodian Palestine (First century AD)
drawn by Constantine Gruber, 1949

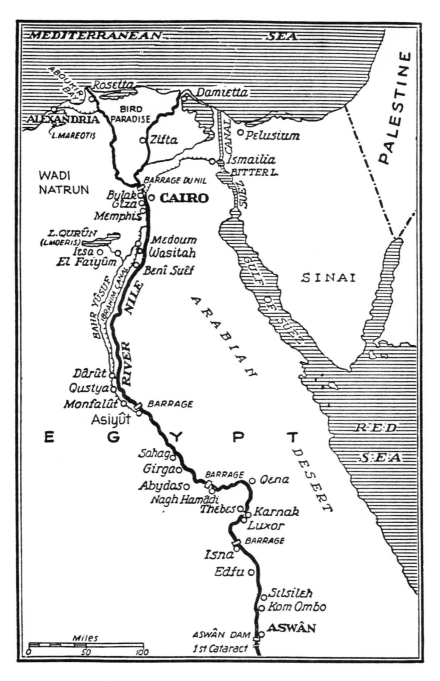

Map of Egypt drawn by Alois Schleyer around 1910
on the basis of memories of the Schleyer expedition, 1874

Editor's Preface

It is always slightly perilous to write about people who have disappeared, to conjure them up as we are doing here. There are nearly always unpredictable results.

And there is no doubt whatsoever about the fact of these disappearances. They have all disappeared: Joseph the Builder, the monks who handed down his story in four volumes, Friedrich Schleyer, the amateur archaeologist who discovered them, Constantine Gruber, the translator, even the original fourth-century codices themselves — disappeared, unaccountably lost. Like the Bogomils or the Khazars or the Seventh Imam, they have been occulted, leaving behind, in each case, the text of this little worm-eaten library and the not insubstantial debris of their dealings with it.

Mar Yusuf, the ancient Coptic monastery from which the Joseph Archive derives, continuously occupied since the fourth century, is today a pillaged, abandoned site in the Fayoum, perennially under threat from the Egyptian government, which — should the funding ever materialize — has plans to create a flood basin in the area.

Schleyer, who pirated away their treasure nearly a century ago, abandoned work on the documents one day, never to be seen again. There were rumors later of suicide in a cheap hotel in Brest.

And Gruber, the last expert to deal with them, deposited his thorough, workmanlike translations in the basement safe of the University of Leipzig library, complete with notes, correspondence, and commentaries — but without the codices themselves — and has been lost to the known world for the past twenty-three years.

I suppose care must be taken when invoking those who have disappeared so mysteriously. One has always to decide whether it might not be better simply to let them remain among the missing, to leave them silent.

But, then, the silence of missing persons has nearly deafened us here in the late unlamented German Democratic Republic. It is 1989 now — the "Spring of Nations." And we are preparing ourselves here in Leipzig for a veritable symphony of openness: open files, open windows, open graves. No doubt, the public will find odd some of the sounds it hears in the process, rising as they do from the throats of those, dead and alive, who have not spoken for a very long time.

But the reader has more pressing concerns. The book he or she has in hand, for example — the Joseph Archive, as we call it — can it be *authentic?* The question naturally arises when a book begins with words like these: "To the sage Jason, light of the Torah in the East, and lover of the poor, from the refugee Joseph in Alexandria"? It is difficult to say. All we have to go by is an unruly stack of translations in a leather suitcase in an old safe stumbled upon during the replacement of a heating duct in the University of Leipzig library basement.

Goodness knows European history abounds in forgeries of ancient documents. There was the business of the highly sentimental "Childhood of Christ" passed off by the French rascal Catulle Mendes in 1894 as an ancient infancy narrative unearthed at the abbey of St. Wolfgang in the Salzkammergut. Then there was a particularly offensive little American product called "The Arhko Volume" pasted together about the same time as the more ingenious "Letter of Benan" forged by Ernst Edler von der Planitz, a work that caused a modest stir in Central Europe in the 1920s.

It deserves to be said that the Joseph Archive was the subject of two intensive forgery trials in the late 1870s. But while the experts failed to establish that the texts were fraudulent, their defenders also failed to demonstrate conclusively that they were not.

Without the original documents — if original documents there were — these paper echoes of "The Gospel of Joseph" will have to stand on their own merits. I am afraid interested readers of our occasional university publications of historic documents will have to take this one as it is — the one certifiable skeleton in the university's closet — the Joseph Archive: once the proud possession of the state's Committee on Religion and Atheism, now, at your service, texts, notes, letters, commentaries, paperclips, everything.

THE EDITOR
University of Leipzig Review
May 29, 1989

Chapter 1

The Chest beneath the Altar

Friedrich Schleyer (1812–78?) was the discoverer of the so-called Joseph Archive, a collection of four nearly complete ancient codices and numerous fragments, found in the Egyptian Fayoum in the fall of 1874. The documents were in the keeping of Mar Yusuf (St. Joseph), an ancient monastic community in the region, then in its final decline.

Schleyer, a philologist by training and a professor at the University of Leipzig, appears to have been persuaded to turn to archaeology by the spectacular success of Constantin von Tischendorff's discovery of the Codex Sinaiaticus at St. Catherine's monastery in 1859. After negotiations with the Mar Yusuf community, Schleyer removed a trunk with the manuscripts to Athens in November 1874 and from there to Leipzig early the following year. Between August and October of that year, Schleyer serialized an edited version of his diaries of the discovery of the Joseph Archive in the liberal journal *Leipziger Merkur.* He appears to have sought to create a sensation by publishing excerpts in several German dailies, but the pessimistic, mildly anti-imperialist tone of the work precluded that. Since the actual diaries have since been lost, Schleyer's "Chest beneath the Altar" articles are the only surviving record of the expedition to the Fayoum.

Leipziger Merkur serial: "The Chest beneath the Altar:
The Story of the Fayoum Discoveries
in Professor Schleyer's Own Words,"
dated August 15–October 10, 1875

The photostat copies from which the following is taken are in only moderately readable condition due to fire damage to the newspaper's files during the bombing of Leipzig in the last months of the Second World War.

August 1, 1874
Alexandria

Our ship docked at Port Said in a dust storm. Moored out in the harbor and waiting for the winds to die down, we watched Egypt spread out before us for hours and checked our supplies.

(Actually, since I've returned from the Orient, I've found myself recommending the procedure to travelers, whether or not there's a weather condition to warrant it. Once ensconced in a good harbor, stay there for a day, scouting the territory, I advise. Take in the terrain before giving yourself to it. Listen to the pulse of the city before you, take its measure, note its smells and the typical movements and preoccupations of its inhabitants. Soon enough, you will be a part of that landscape yourself, part of those very streets, those routines — whether you like it or not, indistinguishable from the rest. And it's not a bad idea to check what you've brought with you to protect yourself from the known dangers. By all means reassure yourself before you confront all that awaits that you cannot anticipate, for which you cannot plan. Yes, in case you hadn't noticed: travel is a kind of warfare.)

Port Said, clean in its simplicity at the edge of the desert, where sand, sea, and sky reflect one another like hall-length mirrors: cold, prehistoric, primordial surfaces upon which modern civilization wobbles like a parasite — a minor nuisance, I suspect, given the great scheme of things.

What is the civilized world looking for here? For metaphysical thrills, I suppose: to savor in Egypt's yellow-gray vastness the dizzying sensation of the utter inconsequentiality of all lives and values. Rather like what death-defying divers who leap off bridges into rivers are looking for, I imagine. It's well known that northern European travelers to Egypt, upon return, become still more obsessive than before about their little routines and about the care and feeding of what they imagine to be theirs.

Two days in the harbor, one outbreak of dysentery among the porters and three bad beds later, we arrive in Alexandria.

For all its notoriety, not much to look at, Alex. A little like Trieste except that there are British everywhere. And tutors. Alex's newest novelty: rogue Europeans posing as language tutors and "experts" who spend the greater part of their time trying to land lucrative positions with wealthy Copts and émigrés. The leisure hours of these "specialists" are ostentatiously devoted to gambling and whoring with the four-penny women. So much for our civilizing influence in Africa!

Be that as it may, we had our first decent meal in weeks in one of the city's small beachfront pensions and, after what passes in this part of the world for a hot bath, settled in to do some intensive planning of the expedition.

Yes, our friend Strosser was right. Despite the distance from the Fayoum, make Alex your base of operations, he told me last year, when the expedition was merely an idea. No need to steam in your own juices down river in Cairo. Here at least, there's fresh air and the sea. In any case, the new railway into the Fayoum makes things much easier all around. Middle Egypt, the land of Sebek, the crocodile god — it's no longer quite the adventure that it once was.

—

August 7
Cairo

Max and I, with my nephew Alois, our aide, met with the Coptic patriarch's secretary, a burly archdeacon named Fadel, in a parlor off the el-Moallaka Church — the so-called Hanging Church — in Old Cairo.

A cigar-colored, chalky dust settles on everything in this hilltop fortress, Fustat, or "Babylon," the Roman outpost out of which teeming Cairo spread.

Time, of course, is of the essence for us. We simply must have completed our survey of Mar Yusuf and the surrounding area by the fall. Funds are available only through January and Max Eastman, our Egypt expert, has only a few months at most here before he must return to Berlin.

Hence, the frustrations mount as the leisurely pace of Egyptian negotiations goes on. We've already lost a week, meeting with the requisite officials, trying to secure the proper permits and travel documents, the letters of introduction, the private assurances. We had, of course, written ahead to expedite the formalities, but arrived only to find that we needn't have bothered to do anything from Europe. Nothing had been arranged here, nothing.

For Max, this is just one more foray into Egypt. For young Alois, this is a youthful escapade. But I've staked my entire career on this expedition. I've gambled all my credibility on this Fayoum enterprise. Should it fail, should I return empty-handed....

And now, Max tells me, the good archdeacon, who is needed merely to draw up two letters, one for the gatekeeper at Mar

Yusuf and one for the abbot, is insisting that we stay two days —
two days! — in Fustat to see the churches.

"Calm down," Max whispers, "drink your tea. All will be well.
If you go on like this, you'll explode."

"Easy for you to say," I snap back.

"Look, Friedrich, this is the East," Max went on. "There's a
reason for all this 'inefficiency.' It has nothing to do with the nonsense one reads about Oriental carelessness about time. Forgive
me for being blunt, but we're thieves here, we Europeans. The
Egyptians are only too well aware of that. They are like a man
whose house has been broken into and who's trying to reason with
his assailants. At the moment, he hasn't the power to stop them,
but he does have the wit to save what he can or to find some way
to use the situation to his advantage. The whole routine is quite
sophisticated, actually. You're a brigand, eager to relieve him of
his treasures. So, what does he do? He stalls, he takes your measure, he tests your cunning, he tries to gauge how difficult it will
be to mislead you. In some cases, seeing that you're a determined
burglar, he decides that a foreign thief may, after all, be preferable
to a local one, or to a hated rich uncle or to the Muslims or to
the Copts. In giving his treasures to a foreigner, he at least has the
satisfaction of knowing that what he can't have, his enemies can't
either. More tea, Friedrich?"

—

August 10
The oasis of Beni-Suef

Notes on the journey from Cairo to Beni-Suef by rail:

Al-Fayoum: the name is Coptic for sea [Phiom], although all we
spy today, mile after mile, is an arid depression in the great West-
ern Desert southwest of Cairo. Everything in Egypt is memory, the
memory not of continuity, as the naive travel writers boast, but of
catastrophic change. How did Max put it: "A landscape formed
by meteors"? Al-Fayoum, "The Sea": earth mirror of an ancient
Pleistocene lake, forty-five meters below sea level.

On the human plane, though, the Fayoum has had a fairly remarkable time of it historically — what with prehistoric hunters,
the worship of river gods, and a large Jewish presence in the third
century B.C. Like Wadi Natrun and Scete down river, it became a

major center of Egyptian Christianity later on. But after the Arab conquest, the region disappeared from imperial maps and slumbered on in its own routines, dominated by the changeless drama of the Nile.

European investment is planned for the region. Naturally. After all, the area farmers continue to plow the earth with traditional crops such as cereals, grapes, olives, figs, dates, honey, cotton, tobacco, and sugarcane as well as the cultivation of that ancient Fayoum specialty: attar of roses.

This despite the taxes of the Turks. I'm told that at farmers' markets, the buyers must pay not only a tax on the purchase of food but are assessed an additional tariff for the privilege of having it weighed. As a result, poverty even in paradise.

I thought of all that as I watched a be-fezzed Turkish official on a train platform at al-Wasitah suck on a fig.

The palette of the Fayoum: a heavy sludge-green robe glinting with mica, its patchwork of irrigation canals sewn against the seam of the great brown Nile. Everywhere the coalblack palm with which the landscape is secured to the sky. The place reeks of the mystery of the disappearance of gods and dinosaurs.

Strange. As Europeans, we're used to thinking of Christianity as a city-dweller's faith. Here, the reverse is true. The more the train speeds south into Middle and Upper Egypt, the more crosses one sees, the more dirty black-garbed monks one spies crowded in among the peasants at village markets.

By nightfall, it has assumed the dimensions of the fantastic: bonfires blaze near and far across the dark landscape. At a waterstop, the passengers watch a crowd of villagers roast a camel over a huge open fire. Square mud houses have cross-symbols cut into the masonry, at night dimly illumined from within by lamplight.

One wonders what sort of Christianity this can be, unenlightened by the intellectual routines of a metropolitan faith and synchronized so deeply, so suspiciously with the rhythms of the earth.

—

August 11
Church of St. Barbara, Beni-Suef

Although I complained about it all the way from Cairo, staying in Beni-Suef for a few days has turned out to be a good idea after all.

The convent where we've been housed is a clean, handsome new building. And with Alois coming down with some kind of fever, we're lucky to have had the sisters to care for him.

And we're eating well at least. Levantine cuisine gets so tiresome. Everything is faux-Béarnaise, quasi-Bolognese. It's enough to drive one wild. Here, in the Fayoum, at last all is simple and fresh and direct — cucumbers and tomatoes seasoned with lemon and oil, huge radishes, spicy green onions, bean soup, stuffed squab, and black Egyptian bread, rough-milled and hearty.

And I must say they've begun making a passable beer in these parts. That's improved my humor considerably. Naturally, the stuff's not sold publicly due to the sensibilities of the local Muslims. But the priests keep barrels in their cellars for their guests.

They told me in Alex not to expect the Coptic clergy to be much better educated than their charges. As the German attaché remarked, "It's the unpromising sons that are slated for the Church, so don't expect high moral character, either" — at least in the monks. The rural parish priests, people said, were a different matter. They had practical problems to solve, so at the very least they had to have a kind of cunning.

The man could have been describing Father Butros, our host. Though not as broadly educated as a typical German or English parson, he's highly cultivated in his own way, with a keen intelligence. This one doesn't miss a trick.

Over brandy on our second night at St. Barbara's, Max and I were rather thoroughly, though politely, interrogated by the man in serviceable French.

And what had brought us all this way to Beni-Suef? Not its charms, surely.

Max explained about the nurse-monks of St. Menas. On his last trip to Egypt four years ago, in connection with some field work in the Delta, he had met a brother from St. Menas, outside Alexandria, who regularly traveled to a monastery in the Fayoum called Mar Yusuf to nurse the elderly monks there. He thought the scholar would find the place interesting. No one, to his knowledge, had ever studied, much less written about it. Max, unfortunately, could not leave his work then to follow up the suggestion.

That, of course, is where I came in, I informed Father Butros. I had a sabbatical year available to me from the University of

Leipzig and managed to pull together some funds to make the expedition. And so here we are.

"And the young boy?" the priest inquired.

"Oh, my nephew Alois. Along for the ride, as they say. Adventure."

"And I would think for you, too, Dr. Schleyer, no? An adventure."

The meaning behind the elaborately polite smile was obvious. "Adventurer" is a bad word in these parts, just one rung removed from "grave robber," I'm told.

"Hiking across the Fayoum in high summer," I mumbled, "hardly an old man's idea of adventure."

Father Butros appeared to enjoy the riposte. Hearty laughter and more brandy.

"I'm here to study," I said evenly.

"But to study what, may I ask?" the priest leaned forward, deadly serious. "There's nothing to study at Mar Yusuf, nothing that I know of, nothing outstanding in the way of art or historical objects that one can't find in a hundred other, more accessible, sites in Egypt. I haven't visited it in years, but I understand that the monks there don't even have a decent library. They're a very, very poor community and most of them are quite old by now. To my knowledge, they've had no young monks join them in decades."

The priest sat back. "You've been badly advised, I'm afraid, very badly advised."

I looked at Max and decided not to tell the priest about the letter.

—

August 13

After determining that we simply couldn't delay getting to Mar Yusuf any longer, we left Alois in the care of Father Butros and the sisters. Last night, luckily, the fever broke, but he's still much too weak to travel.

Because of the intense heat, we set out at twilight for the nearly two-day sojourn to the monastery, guided by a brilliant moon. Father Butros has insisted on sending along one of his own aides, an oasis guide, Tarek, to assist us. To engage in some light espionage is more likely.

Mental etchings: White mules on mercury-colored paths along the Nile; the creak of waterwheels like the sound of a ship, or a galaxy, under sail; the balmy night, close with the smell of coriander.

For some reason, I found myself thinking as we trundled along in the moonlight of the ancient worker colonies that once lined these byways of the Nile: ribbons of freelance laborers, their beds strapped to their backs, straggling in silence from camp to camp, begging for work, for wages, and, for many, even for breath. It was a death march for thousands. According to the ancient historians, these migrant workers hailed from every province in the region; they were Syrians, Parthians, Arabs, Jews — large numbers of Jews from Palestine, refugees of various sorts.

For some reason, I cannot imagine these hordes with voices, but only as silent giants whose gravestones at Thebes and Deir el-Medina bear only the nameless inscription: "poor in spirit."

I talked to the provincial governor of the Fayoum before leaving Beni-Suef. He adds an important detail to Father Butros's objections to our visit to Mar Yusuf.

It seems that the place has had a bad reputation among Orthodox Copts for centuries. Points of doctrine, it seems, although no Church official has been able to charge the monks or their abbot with any specific dogmatic deviations. This accounts, at least in part, for Father Butros's difficulties.

When I asked the provincial governor if he could be more precise, he would volunteer only that the monks of Mar Yusuf were thought to have had Origenist tendencies nearly a thousand years ago.

"And what does that mean?" I queried. "I'm a philologist, not a theologian."

The governor chuckled. "God only knows. The folklore would have it that the monks of Mar Yusuf don't believe in hell."

"That's a relief," I said.

"I agree," he said, smiling. "But more recently — say, in the last century — the controversy was renewed. Visitors from the area who had gone there to pray said that the monks of Mar Yusuf had their own 'traditions,' their own 'practices,' things not done anywhere else. Hence the vague unease people have about the place. People around here — in the rare event that the monastery would come up in conversation at all — call them *sufis*."

"Sufis? But that's the name for Muslim mystics, isn't it?"

"Precisely," he said, lowering his eyes.

By dawn, we had reached the Bahr Yusuf, the Joseph Canal, which follows the ancient course of the Nile into the Wadi al-Ruwayan. There we refreshed our animals and rested until nightfall for the final leg of the journey.

—

August 15
On the road to Itsa

A first glimpse of Mar Yusuf, at dawn. Poorly tended date orchards lead to a Muslim village — El-Bustani, the Garden — under the circumstances, an ironic name. A few mudbrick houses, a scrawny cypress here and there — and that's it. A small mosque with what looks to be a pedestal for a most impressive minaret, which, however, is nowhere to be seen. The village appears churchless. A mangy, half-starved dog absently scours the alleys between the houses.

Without warning the road jogs sharply east and just beyond the lemon trees, over a half-mile stretch of gray sand, it comes suddenly into view: a high rectangular mudbrick fortress, poorly maintained, flanked by date palms. Its walls, at first glance, appear not so much to have crumbled at the edges, but to have been nibbled on. Two limewash-flecked domes crowned with wrought-iron crosses barely crest the walls. High on the parapet a weathered wooden casing hangs precariously, equipped with an invisible pulley with which to lift basket-clutching guests, one by one, through the monastery's only visible entrance.

As we stand there, tying up our animals and getting our bearings after the days of travel, Max points out the large stone platform rising out of the sand before the enclosure — a prayer place facing Mecca to the east, built centuries ago by the monks to accommodate the religious needs of its Muslim workers and the Bedouin who are permitted to refresh their water supplies from the monastic wells.

Mar Yusuf — the Monastery of St. Joseph the Builder, named in honor of the husband of the Virgin Mary, putative father of Jesus, continuously inhabited since the fourth century — stands bathed in the roseate light of early morning and in its own silence. Sleepless nights, bad food, ignorant guides, and peril like a drunk who might put a knife in your ribs for no reason at all, for this: We've come all the way from Europe for this. Perhaps it's the fatigue; but I am sick with disappointment.

The absence of a great vista and the suddenness with which one happens upon it makes Mar Yusuf, for all its aura of mystery, seem common, a first impression strengthened by the erratic crowing of its roosters.

—

August 16

Had to remain encamped before the monastery for more than a day. Yesterday was the Feast of the Assumption of the Virgin and today, it seems, is one of Mar Yusuf's special commemorations — the Feast of the Bath.

"We're in luck," Max laughs. "Sounds as if the monks are treating themselves to a little basic hygiene. That's a reprieve for the modern sensibility. If you've ever spent any time in an Oriental monastery, where soap and water have a bad reputation, you'll appreciate this unexpected boon."

The feasts, it seems, have caused further delays in our being admitted to the monastery. Damned nuisance if you ask me. For one thing, hordes of village children have made life miserable for us, besieging us night and day for sweets and money and throwing stones at our animals when we try to chase them away.

Got the story on the unfinished minaret, though. It seems that the local Muslims try repeatedly to build their prayer tower only to have it collapse. (The problem is certainly the height. The villagers, naturally, want it to peer over the top of the monastery wall.) But the villagers have another explanation. Every time they begin construction, they're sure the monks of Mar Yusuf curse the minaret, bringing it down upon the heads of the builders.

"They have powers, these priests," the Muslims say. Tarek, our guide, told us that the villagers take their sick to Mar Yusuf, believing that Coptic priests know the ancient Egyptian arts of healing.

"And do they?" I asked him.

We were awakened in the early morning hours by our Bedouin. A monk, it seems, had just arrived to escort us into the monastery.

"At this hour?" I said to Max, throwing on some clothes. Even Max, who's spent a great deal of time with Coptic monks, thought it odd, and, the Egypt expert mumbled, he also didn't like the way the Bedouin were acting. "Jittery," he said.

Outside, a clear three-quarter-moon sealed the envelope of the windless night. It was uncanny — the silence. Not even a dog from the village could be heard barking. Aside from the rustling of garments as we hurried along behind a black-robed figure who had not bothered to introduce himself, there was no sound.

The monastery sits in the shadows of the night, its shapes and contours now made familiar by dreams.

To my surprise, we passed by the casement where the basket was lowered to admit visitors into the compound. So, there was another entrance to the monastery, I thought, as we followed our monk-guide into the shadows along the walls.

What a crazy-quilt of masonry, I mused as we huddled along the thirty-foot-high barricade. It had obviously been built with whatever materials were at hand — plundered from other sites most likely — patched and repatched over the ages.

Stout walls are necessary in these parts, even for men of prayer. Max tells me that Bedouin raiders have been the scourge of the Fayoum over the centuries, coming out of the deserts like a wind to plunder the rich farmland. Monasteries are a particularly fond target of such attentions with their barterable treasures.

"That's why the monks traditionally provide food and water for the local Bedouin," Max had once remarked. "In addition to whatever else may be involved, it's an act of self-preservation."

On the south side of the monastery, facing away from the village, we stopped before a tower with a small slit-like passageway hidden at the rear. We had to remove our packs since the width of the passage was wide enough to permit only a relatively slender man inching sideways to pass through — a man without weapons.

Also I couldn't help noticing that here, on the south side of the monastery, upper parts of the wall had crumbled and a crack had opened along one section of the lower courses of stone. Debris had been stuffed into the breaches, but it wasn't likely that that would deter an attacker long.

Suddenly the monastery's situation became painfully clear to us, along with the likely reasons for the abbot's cryptic plea, addressed to Max's Berlin office, June 5, 1874: "Come to the Fayoum without delay. Can we tempt you across the seas with these words: 'I, Joseph, son of Jacob, of the tribe of Judah, of the house of David, King of Israel, place this testament in your hands'?" Max and I had originally thought the monks were venal. Now it was clear that they were desperate.

—

August 22
Alexandria

The past five days have been as turbulent as a Sinai dust storm. It is only now, after a day's rest on the beachfront at Alex, with Max and the manuscripts safely aboard the *Finland* docked in the harbor, that I am able to sketch the epic events that have overtaken us during the past week.

We never did know who the monk was who led us into the enclosure of Mar Yusuf. That was extraordinary because, as Max says, whatever else they may lack from a European standpoint, Coptic monks are the soul of courtesy.

Once inside the wall, we were literally herded at a jog's pace through the compound, past its dark palms and lemon trees, up its cobbled alleys and passageways.

The whole episode was becoming odder by the minute. There were no lanterns lit anywhere that we could see. In the pitch blackness, we were forced to reach for each other, sometimes to stagger hand-in-hand, as in a nightmare. In the upper galleries that ringed the monastic enclosure, no voices, but scuffling could be heard, as if monks were scurrying about in the darkness.

I did see one lighted room to one side of what I assumed to be the church. The chamber had no door, only an odd peak-like arch that revealed some sort of pool filled with water and lit from above by a hanging silver lamp. A baptistry, one thought, or perhaps where the monks of Mar Yusuf bathe, I smiled, on those rare occasions when they indulge nature.

But there was something curious about the bathhouse, if that's what it was. One had a feeling that there was much more to it than hygiene. As we turned the corner, I realized that the waters had been covered with white blossoms.

Our destination was clear at least: It was the monastic church.

The whirlwind Virgil slowed his pace and told our party — myself, Max, and Tarek, the Beni-Suef guide — to wait at the entrance.

It was an awkward moment. Max had objected to having Tarek accompany us on our night escapade. After all, he was reporting to Father Butros, and that could get sticky, depending on what was about to transpire here in Mar Yusuf, say, if antiquities were to be purchased. Father Butros clearly suspected something of the sort and could make difficulties later on when we tried to smuggle them out of the country.

Max slipped Tarek some coins, with a promise of more later on if he would wait for us here, outside the church.

The monk reappeared with a lighted candle and, regaining a little composure along with his breath, bowed to us with a sheepish smile and gestured in the direction of the door.

Inside, all was mystery.

Frescoes, mostly flaked away, covered the three domes of the apse, or alcove, while, in typical Coptic style, the sanctuary itself was hidden behind ornate inlaid wooden screens. While I had little time to examine the building, one detail caught my eye. Directly behind the altar, in the middle apse, appeared to be the gold-gilt fresco of a large tree of some sort crowned with stars or medallions. The painting stood out because it was the only fresco that had been restored. An unusual design. I'd never seen anything like it in a Coptic church before. What was more, Max said he hadn't either when we talked about it later.

There was no time to do anything but take the sketchiest mental notes, however. Our guide was ushering us in the direction of a tall monk who was standing before the altar, his back to us. There was a single large candle lit in the sanctuary. Otherwise the place was dark.

The altar was covered with a black cloth trimmed in gold, which glimmered in the dim candlelight. One thought instinctively that had all of this been experienced in the full light of day, it might have seemed sullen, oppressive even. But in the light of the one candle, all the black and gold and crimson in view had a warm, intimate splendor.

We stood a long time at the entrance to the sanctuary before the figure turned to face us. Imagine our surprise: the countenance of the priest before us was literally a mask of grief. . . .

[*Editor's note:* The only known copy of Schleyer's *Leipziger Merkur* article breaks off at this point. At least two columns of text appear to be missing. Fortunately, the account of the expedition can be adequately, if more prosaically, filled in by means of an excerpt from the transcript of Max Eastman's testimony given at Schleyer's first forgery trial in Breslau, September 8, 1877.]

Hearing in the Prussian State Court, Breslau

Case No. 33991:
University of Breslau versus Friedrich Schleyer
Records, Vol. 12, Transcript 1139, pp. 56–68

PROSECUTOR: ... Mr. Eastman, please be as precise as you can. You and Professor Schleyer both claim that the abbot of Mar Yusuf — what was his name?

EASTMAN: Pambon. Abbot Pambon.

PROSECUTOR: Ah, yes ... that Abbot Pambon addressed some words to you that night, the night you claim to have spent in the monastic enclosure of Mar Yusuf.

EASTMAN: He did.

PROSECUTOR: All right. To the best of your ability then, will you kindly tell us about that conversation, the one you and Professor Schleyer claim to have had with the abbot? Do not summarize, please. Tell us everything, in as much detail as you can manage.

EASTMAN: To the best of my recollection, these are the words of Pambon, Abbot of Mar Yusuf, to Professor Friedrich Schleyer and myself on the morning of August 17, 1874:

"Gentlemen ... "

PROSECUTOR: Wait. In what language did he address these words to you?

EASTMAN: In French.

PROSECUTOR: Not in Arabic?

EASTMAN: No. In French of a bookish sort, but not impossible to follow.

PROSECUTOR: I see. You, Mr. Eastman, speak Arabic, I take it?

EASTMAN: Yes, of course.

PROSECUTOR: Continue.

EASTMAN: " . . . Gentlemen," the abbot began, "forgive us for rousing you at a strange hour to impart an even stranger greeting. But understand that for the sons of Joseph these are strange times. This is a night of poverty: We cannot so much as offer you our hospitality nor even the leisure to discuss fully the reasons why we urged you to come to us. Like the children of Israel, it is a Passover night for us when the angel of death is abroad and when what can be done must be done quickly."

PROSECUTOR: Remarkable. It's been how long since this incident?

EASTMAN: A little more than three years.

PROSECUTOR: Is your memory always this reliable, Mr. Eastman?

EASTMAN: It was an extraordinary moment, sir. One tends to remember those.

PROSECUTOR: Of course. Then what happened?

EASTMAN: At this point, Abba Pambon summoned several monks to remove the altar covering. Once that was done, a brass star set in gray marble could be seen beneath the altar. Two of the monks turned the seal — not without great difficulty — and then lifted the marble slab onto the sanctuary floor, revealing a crypt or perhaps a small cave beneath the church. We couldn't see much of it, you understand, from our vantage point. The monks lowered themselves into it. . . .

PROSECUTOR: Hold on. Where did all these other monks come from? We began with just two monks, the abbot and the guide, did we not? Now we have all these other gentlemen in the picture.

EASTMAN: I couldn't tell you.

PROSECUTOR: What can't you tell us?

EASTMAN: Where they all came from. Things that night were happening so fast. Naturally, our attention — Professor Schleyer's and mine — was focused on what the abbot was doing. Suddenly there were all these other monks about. I supposed they'd been summoned somehow.

PROSECUTOR: You heard no bell?

EASTMAN: Coptic monasteries don't have them, sir. If you will recall, Ottomans have long forbidden church bells to Christians under their rule. For the most part, wooden clappers beaten with a stick take the place of bells in the Near East. A most distinctive sound. We heard nothing of the sort that night.

PROSECUTOR: I feel bound to say that what you've told us differs somewhat from Professor Schleyer's account, but no matter. There will always be different recollections in these affairs, won't there? Continue. You were telling us about the underground chamber...

EASTMAN: Yes. Two monks lowered themselves into it.

PROSECUTOR: What was the abbot doing all this while?

EASTMAN: The abbot and the other monks prostrated as soon as the cave had been entered.

PROSECUTOR: They got down on all fours, you mean.

EASTMAN: That's what I mean, yes. After several minutes, the monks emerged with a wooden chest with brass mountings that they placed before the abbot.

PROSECUTOR: Was the chest you describe new or old?

EASTMAN: New.

PROSECUTOR: You're sure about that.

EASTMAN: Quite sure.

PROSECUTOR: Hm. What happened next?

EASTMAN: While the monks sang some sort of hymn, the abbot rose and summoned us to the entrance to the sanctuary.

PROSECUTOR: You and Professor Schleyer?

EASTMAN: That's right. Friedrich was particularly impressed by their singing, as I remember. (Myself, I'm no great admirer of the music of the East.) But Friedrich was really taken with the low dissonant droning of the monks. He talked about it frequently once we'd set sail for Europe. "Close your eyes and you could imagine yourself breathing fourth-century air," he'd...

PROSECUTOR: Nice touch, these details, Mr. Eastman, so full of atmosphere. But let's keep the story moving, shall we?

EASTMAN: Right. Abba Pambon took out a large key from his belt and opened the chest. He motioned Friedrich and me to come closer. At first it was difficult to see what it was that he was drawing out of the chest for us to look at. It wasn't until I'd reached the top of the steps separating the sanctuary from the nave of the church that I got a good look at what it was.

PROSECUTOR: And...?

EASTMAN: It was a large codex, sir. By the way it was bound I knew immediately that what we had before us was a fourth-century document. The abbot opened it to a page...

PROSECUTOR: For the record, would you please tell the court what a "codex" is, Mr. Eastman?

EASTMAN: Certainly. It's a bound book, a collection of pages stitched together, replacing in Late Antiquity the scroll and the wax tablet.

PROSECUTOR: In other words, the book as we know it today.

EASTMAN: Correct.

PROSECUTOR: Mr. Eastman, I don't doubt your expertise — though, I must say, your curriculum vitae does not do you justice in that respect. But did you say just now that you knew at once that the codex the abbot held in front of you was of fourth-century vintage?

EASTMAN: I did. I knew from the way it was bound.

PROSECUTOR: I see.

EASTMAN: We don't have many of these early codices around — two to be exact — the Codex Sinaiaticus and the Codex Alexandrinus, both of the Greek Bible. So one would tend to notice a thing like that.

PROSECUTOR: Two early codices did you say? But shouldn't it be three? How can you have forgotten the Codex... Iosephicus, the "Joseph Codex," the one you have brought into the world, Mr. Eastman?

EASTMAN: I'm coming to that, sir.

PROSECUTOR: I'm sure you are. Proceed.

EASTMAN: The abbot opened the codex to a page — the text was clearly in Coptic — and translated into French the words: "With the permission of all involved, including the council of royal priests in Bethlehem, I'm depositing in your care this dossier on the circumstances surrounding the birth of my son Joshua...."

PROSECUTOR: Let the record show that Mr. Eastman is quoting from the documents in question, from...

EASTMAN: ... the Joseph Letters.

PROSECUTOR: You'll pardon us for referring to it as Exhibit 1. Go on.

EASTMAN: At this point, the monk who had escorted us from our encampment came forward with a candle to allow us to examine the manuscript. While Friedrich pored over the codex, I investigated the contents of the chest, which included three other apparently complete codices and a handful of fragments bound in new leather. The whole collection appeared to be in excellent condition.

PROSECUTOR: For approximately how long did you go on examining the documents?

EASTMAN: For around twenty minutes, I'd say.

PROSECUTOR: Let's see if I have this straight: that's one, two, three, four complete fourth-century codices we're talking about, right? Not a bad night's work, Mr. Eastman, seeing that it took Tischendorff nearly fifteen years and barrels of European cash to pry the Codex Sinaiaticus loose....

EASTMAN: May I continue.

PROSECUTOR: By all means. I digress.

EASTMAN: We were — Friedrich and I — as you gentlemen will surely understand, ecstatic about the discovery.

PROSECUTOR: Naturally.

EASTMAN: But just as we were about to suggest to the abbot that we repair to the monastery library or some other quiet place to examine the documents further, perhaps even to begin a rough catalogue, Abba Pambon replaced the documents and closed the chest.

PROSECUTOR: Just like that?

EASTMAN: Yes.

PROSECUTOR: No doubt the good abbot explained himself?

EASTMAN: As a matter of fact, he did. "Forgive us, gentlemen," he said, "we have no more time now. We should not have delayed this long, but we wanted you to be assured that these documents exist before we demanded something from you in their regard.

"As the Holy Joseph, author of these letters, once deposited this dossier in the care of Jason of Alexandria, we, full of sorrow, are compelled — for a season — to place them in your care."

He went on to explain that Bedouin raiders had been spotted crossing the Bahr Yusuf that morning. "They raid at dawn," he said.

Apparently, they had been safe from such raids for decades because of the esteem in which the community was held by the local Bedouin. But the local chieftains had gotten themselves embroiled in a range war with a Sudanese clan — a war they were losing. It was only a matter of time until victorious horsemen, in hot pursuit, pillaged the ancestral lands of the vanquished.

"We had hoped to avoid this until we were better prepared,"

he said. "The ground beneath our southern wall has shifted. We stand exposed."

"What the Holy Joseph has written cannot be allowed to fall into alien hands. What the Bedouin do not burn for fuel, they will disperse to the merchants of Alexandria."

He urged that there was not a moment to lose. "You must take the chest at once," he cried. "Take the books to Europe where they will be safe. You yourselves must return by another route across the canal. We will direct you."

PROSECUTOR: Well done, Mr. Eastman. Nicely rehearsed. I doubt that there was a preposition in that last speech that didn't also appear in Professor Schleyer's deposition. Well, with one exception: "For a season" — that's an interesting phrase. Professor Schleyer never mentioned that idea. Will you go over that part of the abbot's remarks again, please?

EASTMAN: The part about being compelled to place the documents in our care for a season?

PROSECUTOR: Yes, that's it. What did you take the words to mean, Mr. Eastman?

EASTMAN: That, I suppose, in the Mar Yusuf community's view, the documents were on loan, so to speak?

PROSECUTOR: On loan?

EASTMAN: Until the danger had passed.

PROSECUTOR: Ah, I see, a condition, in effect, attached to your ... possession of the documents.

EASTMAN: I suppose so. I seem to recall that the abbot even said something more directly about that.

PROSECUTOR: Such as?

EASTMAN: "Word will come."

PROSECUTOR: I beg your pardon?

EASTMAN: "Word will come." I took him to mean that at some future date, when Mar Yusuf had been reconstituted as a community, he or another authorized representative would contact us about the documents — about their return to Egypt.

PROSECUTOR: Interesting. Can you think of a reason why Professor Schleyer should omit such an important detail — a condition attached to your possession and, therefore, certainly the *sale* of any of these alleged antiquities?

EASTMAN: I cannot speak for Professor Schleyer.

PROSECUTOR: No. But you will admit, will you not, that, legally speaking, Professor Schleyer would appear to hold these documents in trust — at least according to what you have told us?

EASTMAN: I suppose that's right.

PROSECUTOR: Thank you, Mr. Eastman. You have been very helpful. Let's wrap things up, shall we? What happened after that, after the abbot entrusted you and Professor Schleyer with the alleged codices?

EASTMAN: Heeding the abbot's warning, we left that very night with the chest. By dawn, we had crossed the Joseph canal and were out of the area. We heard reliable reports from scouts on the canal that Abba Pambon had been right to take precautions. A dawn raiding party had, in fact, attacked the monastery and plundered the village. Three years ago we were told by Alexandrian sources that Mar Yusuf was, at present, for all intents and purposes, abandoned. That fact has not been independently confirmed.

PROSECUTOR: An ending, if I may say so, sir, worthy of a cheap romantic novel. A little too neat for my taste. What about the professor's nephew left in Beni-Suef? We appear to have several versions of that strand of the story.

EASTMAN: No mystery there as far as I'm concerned. Fearing complications in Beni-Suef, Professor Schleyer went alone to fetch his nephew Alois there while I remained with the codices and the rest of our party at the oasis of Al-Wasitah. From there we made our way back to Alexandria where we boarded ship for Europe....

Editor's Afterword on the Fate of Friedrich Schleyer

Not much is known about the death of Schleyer. The only evidence we have is a begging letter he wrote to his former associate Max Eastman from a Brest hotel in 1878. In the letter, he threatened suicide.

What reduced the philologist to this state is clear: After returning to Leipzig with the Joseph Archive in 1875, Schleyer, much to his dismay, found himself and his treasure upstaged by the great number of important Egyptian finds of that season. In addition, forgeries of ancient documents had begun circulating in Europe, fed by the growing popular interest in the Near East and its treasures. The forgeries created an environment in the academic community suspicious of Schleyer and Eastman's brand of freelance archaeology.

Hoping to establish his fame by means of the codices, Schleyer exhausted his funds setting up lecture tours and publishing preliminary translations of the documents. But what finally broke him were the two forgery trials held in 1877–78, instituted when Schleyer, in desperate financial straits, tried to sell the "Prayer of Joseph in the Mikveh," one of the Mar Yusuf fragments — missing, by the way, from this collection — to the University of Breslau. This final, and inconclusive, effort to establish the antiquity of his documents caused him to deed the whole archive to the University of Leipzig library and to focus all his energies on dodging a growing army of creditors.

Chapter 2

The Alexandrian Epistles

Editor's note: The following translation of the Alexandrian Epistles is by Fredrich Schleyer (hereafter FS); it has been thoroughly reworked and updated on the basis of new research by Constantine Gruber (hereafter CG).

The typewritten copy of the translation, from which the following was taken, was the property of Martin Niebel, director of the Leipzig University Institute for the Study of Religion and Atheism.

Translators' Introduction

The Alexandrian Epistles consist of the nearly complete text of six ancient letters attributed to Joseph, husband of the Virgin Mary and putative father of Jesus of Nazareth. The documents have been conclusively dated to the fourth century A.D. and are written in the Coptic tongue. But persuasive internal evidence leads one to believe that they are translations from earlier Greek originals [FS]. The precise date of this Greek "source text" cannot be determined at the present time [CG]. There appear to be occasional interpolations from later periods when the epistles had become a formative spiritual legacy for the monks of Mar Yusuf. These "Josephite" glosses are clearly marked by brackets — thus [...] — in the text of the epistles.

Typewritten note, dated May 29, 1949,
from Joseph Archive Project Coordinator Constantine Gruber
to his supervisor, Martin Niebel

The following note was attached to the translations by paperclip.

From: CG
To: The "Boss"
Re: You Know

You will note, Martin, that I've dropped the "von" from my name. As you rightly suggested, I'd be much better off as simple Constantine Gruber than drawing undue attention from members of the committee with the aristocratic "von." Most people, of course, could care less, but then, as you said, why give an enemy a pretext for mischief? What would I do without you, I wonder?

Now I know your impatience and the impatience of our col-
leagues at the Institute. I'm aware that you want results. "Just
as soon as it will hold up in 'court.'" Weren't those your words,
Martin? I know you all believe that what we've uncovered here
in a library basement may well be the Qumran scrolls of Europe.
But then we can't say we know much about the nature of that little "find" at this point either now, can we — the scrolls found at
Qumran near the Dead Sea? Mostly rumors, my friend, from our
efficient intelligence services in Amman.

Hype notwithstanding, it will be years before we really know
if some Bedouin shepherd has unwittingly "blown" Christianity's
cover with those scrolls. For godssake, we don't even know how
many there are, let alone whether or not some of them are not
dark with age but with a little Arabian tea. Know what I mean?

Now as for our own little treasure, at least, we're sure these
are authentic ancient documents. And, unlike the Qumran trove,
they've been well cared for. They're in amazingly good condition — especially this first text, these six letters.

Anyway, Martin, I have to be polite with the committee. But,
between us, I want it clearly understood that I'm here as a
scholar — the only Coptologist East of Berlin, in fact — not as
a propagandist for the Ministry for the Triumph of Godlessness.
I'm as interested as anybody else in the "new world order." But
scholarship — real scholarship — takes time. And I simply can't
guarantee a propaganda coup for the committee.

For starters, we don't really know what we're dealing with here,
with these documents of Schleyer's. He was full of hearty Lutheran
pessimism, but it's just possible — despite the "atmosphere" of
scholarly reticence — that he really believed in the historicity
of the Joseph Archive, that he entertained the thought that he
had actually stumbled upon something in the Fayoum ultimately
traceable to the family of Jesus of Nazareth.

But what I'm working with is these fourth-century monastic
texts. Please, my friend, stress that point to Herr Toppler: We
don't have a clue as to what, if anything, these letters have to do
with Christ or his family. As far as scholarship is concerned, that's
not even important. I know that's not what the committee wants
to hear, but...

I can hear you now: Throw me a crumb, Stanz. I've got to give
the committee something! Okay. Tell them this: Beyond the sig-

nificance of the documents for Coptic studies — and I know how the committee cares about that! — what's intriguing about them is that some of the texts at least are clearly translations of older documents. That becomes clearer to us every day. How much older, of course, will take a little time to determine. Months . . . dare I say years?

You asked me about Joseph, the central character of the texts, the other day. Well, it's pretty early in the process for precise identifications. Looking at these documents is a lot like a coroner trying to determine the identity of a murder victim from a few scattered body parts. (Tell that to Toppler: wasn't he the Leipzig Regional Coroner before the war, before politics, before the invention of fire?) The monks at Mar Yusuf called these six epistles "The Holy Letters." (It was Schleyer who dubbed them — rather grandly, don't you think? — the Alexandrian Epistles.) And the monks, presumably, believed that Joseph, the putative father of Jesus of Nazareth, had actually written them.

However, it's not clear who this "Joseph" was, Martin. Might have been anyone — or no one. It was common in ancient times to disguise a social critique for which one could be made to suffer exquisitely under the pious cloak of some unimpeachable (and safely dead) authority.

One of my researchers (Julia, the redhead, the one you . . . well, perhaps I shouldn't commit *that* to paper; she has "access") has suggested that the specific references to New Testament events may have been interpolated later to "Christianize" a pre-existing, and rather colorful, set of Augustan period letters.

Nevertheless, whatever they are, they've got some splendid stuff in them — I mean, purely from a literary point of view. They're more than worth all the effort we're putting into the project.

But, Martin, tell the committee that answers aren't easy to come by. See for yourself.

GRUBER

EPISTLE I

TO THE SAGE JASON,
light of the Torah in the East
and lover of the poor,
from the refugee Joseph
in Alexandria:

Shalom.

I, Joseph, son of Jacob, of the tribe of Judah, of the house of David, King of Israel, place this testament in your hands, Jason, learned friend of my exile, counsellor of my soul. I do this not for the glory of my name or of my house, but for the glory of God, that the truth be known by a prudent man until the hour that the Holy One has appointed for vindication.

I write this for you, light of Alexandria, from the Fayoum where I have just completed the work for the villa of the Greek Diogenes, my last commission in Egypt.[1]

As you see, what I have written is in another and more elegant hand — not my rough-hewn Greek, not my tradesman's scrawl. Simon, the mute, the unfortunate whose tongue was removed by Enobarbus, son of Agathodorus, tyrant of Pelusium, has seen fit to cover the shame of an unworldly education — may God avenge his sorrows — with the garment of an Alexandrian wit.

(You will doubtless rebuke me for this extravagance. "Why scribes and parchments when a simple message, folded over in the Roman style and in your own hand, would give me more pleasure? Better yet, if you do not return through the capital, why not say farewell through one of your workmen?" I can hear you say the words, rabbi. But in taking leave of Egypt, I have things of great importance to commend to you — facts with which I wish you to be familiar. Communications of importance beg to be flattered, don't they? They require their little ceremonies.)

---

1. This Joseph was what we would call today a building contractor. Like other skilled and unskilled labor in Roman Egypt, he would have migrated up the Nile from one workers' colony to another looking for freelance employment. —CG

In any case, what father among us would spare any expense in securing the welfare of his children?

> And it is a child's honor that I commend to you, great one,
> a child you know, O light of Alexandria,
> a child born in a cave.

I have been silent about this business for three years now, even though I've not been ignorant of the complaints about me in Alexandria: the questions that have been raised about the child, about the circumstances of the marriage of his parents, about the origins of the notoriety said to be attached to this particular family of exiles. Yes, eminence, I've long known that certain eminent Judeans have approached you over the years, suggesting that your generosity toward us compromises you in some way. "You must be made aware of these rumors," they will have urged. After all, so much of the revenue for Alexandria's charities, Alexandria's many hospitalities is dependent on the voluntary contributions, therefore the goodwill, of Judean traders. (The Nile, dear friend, though long, bears news of that nature more swiftly than doves.)

If these had been the complaints of mere tradesmen, I'm confident that you would have spurned their tales out of hand. But the words of men like Menelaus of Gilo are less easy to dismiss, even for you. Menelaus, after all, is not only a man of means and reputation but a relative of mine.

(He's also a native of Gilo, it must be added, the town made famous by Ahithopel, King David's false counselor, of whom it is written: "When he saw that his counsel was not acted upon, he hanged himself on a tree.")[2]

But what reason could the eminent merchant have for maligning his own cousin? Indeed. If weighty men make weighty charges, they leave their mark, even on the smoothest of brows.

Nevertheless, although I'm sure you have had your fill of their tales, you, O Dove of Egypt, have never failed to greet us openly in the synagogue, to recommend this poor craftsman to the notables of Alexandria, to bless my wife and child, to call me to the *bima* to read the Holy Torah, or even to invite me to your *haburah* — to the intimate fellowship of your disciples. You have never once asked for an explanation.

---

2. 2 Sam. 17:23. —FS

No wonder the locals say that "Jason has a dove's tongue." After my wife — who, as you know, shuns slander like a disease — I have never known a person whose speech is as pure as yours, as free of that curse of the heart — the love of another's shame.

For my part, I shall — indeed, must — remain silent about these matters. But not from you. With the permission of all involved, including the council of the royal priests in Bethlehem, I'm depositing in your care this dossier on the circumstances surrounding the birth of my son, Joshua. Have I not confided to you from time to time even my most secret thoughts? Shall I who do not fear your worst quail before your virtue?

Yet this is essential, old friend: All that I tell you must lay buried with you as in a tomb. As the Psalmist says, "O Lord, set a guard over my mouth, a watch over my lips."[3] This must stand as a kind of covenant between us. Should you not wish to take on the burden of this silence, father, read no further. Simon's son, Menachem, will call on you in a few days and you may give him the five sealed letters that remain.

And as to the reputation of the child, this suffices for us: One day his word will rise.

Until then, this, and much more, remains between us.

๛

Do you remember how surprised you were to see us on that very first day — my wife Miriam, my son Joshua — dumped like so many bags of grain at the synagogue door by the Gaza traders? (With what little complaint you paid our ransom. You knew, of course, that they had no right to extract more money from you on our account. They had been amply paid in Gaza for their services. But we, alas, hadn't a drachma more to give them.)

"Where have you come from, son?" These were your first words to us as I stepped forward to greet you, the white dust of the Sinai still on my face.

I had no idea that you were a sage, then, much less the prince of our people in Alexandria, the head of the Jewish community. Indeed, how was I to know? The rabbis of Jerusalem with their prayer shawls like tents allow no one the privilege of ignoring them. But you, the most famous preacher in Egypt, known as far

---

3. Ps. 141:3. —FS

as the Lebanon, the master to whom even Gentiles come for wisdom, the envy, Alexandrians say, even of the Greeks, you were hardly better dressed than I, a refugee, and fourteen days in the desert at that!

If I had known then that I was speaking with Jason of Alexandria...well, I would hardly have begun our friendship with a joke, would I?

Do you remember? "I am Joseph, your brother," I said with a grin, the greeting my holy namesake, Joseph the Dreamer, sold by his brothers to Egyptian traders, gave when he revealed himself. I think I even dared to mimic the way we cantillate those words in the synagogue as I embraced you. With your Egyptian sobriety, you must have found all these antics a little trying.

But then the accent had to have told you that you were dealing with Galileans. And, when in trouble, what else would a Galilean do but crack jokes!

Late that night, under Alexandria's bright warm sky, in the synagogue courtyard where we were bedded down, you paid us a visit. Do you remember? Of course, I knew who you were by then. (We had heard of your fame even in a place like Kefar Nazrat, where I had lived since my father, Jacob, died.)

The sky was blue as a particularly fine tidal pearl, as the eye of Lake Mareotis in the moonlight. It was the kind of light that, they say, causes one to see hidden meanings in texts if one reads by it.[4]

By then, Miriam lay asleep on a mat against the courtyard wall, the child curled up in the crook of her arm. For a while, once the evening prayer had concluded, I too had taken my place beside her.

But sleep would not descend. For a long time, until you came, dear friend, I sat, propped up against a courtyard pillar, unable to take my eyes off them — the bride and the child.

Worries crowded my thoughts: How long could we hope to stay here under the protection of the community, would I find work, would Miriam and the child be safe? But, even so, these worries were a kind of buzzing in the ear, a mere nuisance before the riv-

---

4. Lake Mareotis is a salt water lake south of Alexandria at the boundary between the delta and the desert. It was framed in ancient times by the Ptolemaic city of Taposiris where there was a great temple dedicated to Osiris and the first in a chain of lighthouses that stretched down the north African coast from Alexandria to Cyrene (today's Libya). —CG

eting face of their beauty: the beauty of the bride and the child. How I loved to stand guard over them at night: To love them with my eyes until I felt I would burst.

"You need your rest, Joseph." Suddenly I felt your hand on my shoulder.

"Rabbi," I said, jumping to my feet.

Restraining my attempt to render homage to a sage, you sat down with me in the darkness, joining my vigil.

For a long time, the two of us remained in silence. Now both of us were watching them, listening to the sound of their breathing, joined, in the distance, by the sound of the Roman sea.

After a long time, knowing that you were waiting for me to speak, I began to tell you how we came to be in this place, why I had swept down the Sorek Valley with my family one night disguised as Bedouin, why, like thousands of refugees before us, we had dared the perils of the wilderness.

We talked then, you and I, until the firstlight. Only then I did not tell you the whole story.

Now, Jason, light of Alexandria, I will tell you everything.

Excursus on the Legend of St. Jason of Alexandria
by Constantine Gruber

Jason of Alexandria (c. 38 B.C.–? A.D.) was the head of the Jewish community in Alexandria during the greater part of the Augustan age (44 B.C.–A.D. 20), a period that saw the rise of Roman rule over Egypt, Jewish self-government in the Greek cities of Egypt, and the Jewish-Greek riots in Alexandria. Scion of an ancient Alexandrian family that could trace its roots in Egypt back six centuries, Jason was the great grandson of one of the Septuagint translators and the father of Philo Judaeus, Hellenistic Judaism's greatest thinker. That the family had fabulous wealth at its disposal is clear from the fact that during Herod the Great's reconstruction of the Temple complex in Jerusalem they furnished all the gold plate for one of the Temple gates. Even more than his famous son, Jason was noted for his homilies and commentaries on the Scriptures. While virtually nothing of Jason's own writings have come to light, the irenic nature of his work may be inferred from the fact that even the Greeks called him "The Bridge" — one who made efforts to reconcile Alexandria's warring intellectual and ethnic worlds. Should these epistles prove authentic, they add yet another dimension — his tireless concern for Jewish refugees — to our estimation of the man. Jason lived to see his son Phinehas confirmed as head of the Jewish community in Alexandria and, it is said, to witness Philo's disastrous embassy to Caligula in A.D. 40, although it is likely the elder sage had already died by then. The tradition of Mar Yusuf has it that Jason was martyred by Caligula's agents in Alexandria as a secret Christian, but that seems clearly apocryphal. The story first appears in a fragment from a ninth-century Coptic martyrology found at the monastery of St. Menas and currently stored at the Graeco-Roman Museum in Alexandria. A highly corrupted version of that text made its way into Mar Yusuf's medieval "Life of St. Jason of Alexandria." Among Professor Schleyer's effects were found a die-shaped talisman supposedly containing a piece of the rabbi/martyr's tongue.

"The Life of St. Jason of Alexandria" compiled by Constantine Gruber

Note: Below find an account of the life of Jason of Alexandria compiled from translations of two separate, but related, fragments appended to the codices:

- a ninth-century Coptic martyrology that constitutes the first literary reference to the legend of the martyrdom of St. Jason of Alexandria. While the martyrdom story borrows freely from the classic models, the mention in it of St. Jason of Alexandria as an anchorite is not quite so far-fetched as it seems. Recent evidence from the so-called Qumran scrolls as well as other ancient authorities demonstrate that Jewish, Hellenistic, and Hermetic circles had anchorites, that is, solitaries who "withdrew" for contemplation.

- fragments of the medieval "Life of St. Jason of Alexandria."

Bracketed words have been inserted by the compiler, Constantine Gruber.

৵

... on the island of Pharos, where the Seventy had first [rendered] the Word of God [the Hebrew Scriptures] into the Word of men [the common tongue, Greek], on the isthmus of light, [where] a lamp [was once] raised in the house of idols [the Septuagint translation of the Bible, LXX], Jason contemplated the mysteries of God.[5]

(How favored is the one who devotes himself to the things of God in his youth from the first hour, who labors in the full heat of the day, when the heart is strong and the blood full of desire. That one will find full pardon for sin. That one will be loved by heaven. [text missing]. . . . When the years multiply, the heart sick with the bitterness of life, the body asleep, the vigor fading, who will fail then, at the eleventh hour, to turn to God, seeing that he has exhausted all other hopes?)

He lived in one of the blessed huts [of the LXX rabbis], in the shadow of the great Light [the Pharos], subsisting on the dates that grew there and drawing his water from the well outside the fortress. And he lacked for nothing.

As it is written: "The desire for wisdom is a kingdom." And in another place it is written: "He who watches for her at dawn shall not be disappointed, for he shall find her sitting by his gate."[6]

At night, navigators [in those days] saw two great lights shining from the island, [one from the] tower and one from Jason's hut. "Someone has lit a bonfire on the island," [they informed officials], "and the light of the bonfire is even greater than that of the beacon. . . ."[7]

. . . They, of course, failed to understand that the torch was merely physical fire, while the light that burned in the heart of Jason was the flame of the Logos.[8]

(Flee, Christian soul, flee from the world of the great tower, the world of appearances, to the hut of the Spirit, to the inner cham-

---

5. The author indulges himself in puns here on the fact that the Septuagint (the "lamp raised in the house of idols") was traditionally supposed to have been composed on the island where Ptolemy Philadelphius built the great Pharos lighthouse in the third century B.C. —CG

6. These quotations are rather free renderings from the Book of the Wisdom of Solomon, an Alexandrian work of about 100 B.C.: Wisdom 6:18, 6:14. —CG

7. Here, apparently, there was an account of the officials' investigation of the reports and the finding of Jason alone at his meditations. —CG

8. Logos, or "The Word." Like the Alexandrian notion of "Sophia," or Divine Wisdom, the Logos concept proposed a "bridge" linking God and man; employed by Philo Judaeus, Alexandrian Judaism's greatest philosopher. —CG

ber where wisdom makes men friends of God, bridging the great
gulf, in whose light all other light is shadow.)

There, in the shadow of the lighthouse, Jason discovered this
phrase, which he repeated day and night: "In the beginning was
the Word, in the beginning was the Word . . . "[9]
[*Note:* We are missing most of the rest of the MS., which goes on
to document the later persecution of the young Jason's teaching in
Alexandria. This appears to be an account inserted at a much later
date than the "anchorite" verses. It seems to end with Jason being
tortured by Alexandrian opponents, perhaps by having his tongue
torn out. Clearly, it is a variant on the standard legend that Jason
was so mutilated. —CG]

EPISTLE II

Let me begin at the beginning, where it all started, under the oak
tree that still shades the old bridle path from Nazareth to Rakkah,
on the way to the Sea of Galilee.

Yes, beloved sage, that oak tree, the one whose image now
adorns the wooden doors of the Aron ha-Kodesh, the Holy Ark,
of your synagogue, the one I carved there, at your bidding, with
the symbols of the twelve tribes of Israel in its branches and a star
in the heart of the tree for the Messiah. You might say that it is a
family design — the oak tree flecked with stars. I carved a similar
one for the house of studies in Nazareth.

But the story really began the day I saw Miriam, daughter of
Joachim, gathering spices there.

My family, as you know, is Bethlehemite, Judean, of the house
of David the King. Our genealogy can be traced all the way back
to our father Abraham, who sanctified many oaks in Israel.

There is a legend in our clan that in each of our generations,
there will be one man and one woman, members of one of our
families, who are prepared secretly by God for the creation of the
Messiah. As it is written in the Book of the Prophet, "A shoot shall
come out from the stump of Jesse and a branch shall grow out of
his roots."[10]

---

9. Logos, "The Word"; we have echoes here of the prologue to the Gospel of John
(John 1:1). —CG
10. Isa. 11:1. —FS

This man and this woman in each generation shall be the hidden conduit of the Messiah's seed in each generation until the day of his revelation to Israel.

The identity of the couple is known only to our council of priests. As I say, it is a tradition in our family. There are other branches of the royal house, it must be said, that have similar family legends, seeing that it is from us that the Messiah will spring — may his coming be in our days.

You will doubtless wish to know something of the procedure — how our sages determine who the candidates are.

It is done in this way. When a child, male or female, is born to us they are taken by their parents to the local family priest. A lamb is killed, and there is a three-day feast in the child's honor. During the festivities, when the parents come privately to receive the priest's blessing, the sage, as in the ancient times, as in the days of Aaron the priest and Shmuel the prophet, takes out the urim and thummim — the sacred dice — and tosses them on a scarlet cloth before the child.

This is as the History of the Kings of Israel says when it describes how the choice of the kingship fell on Saul of the clan of Matri when the prophet Shmuel cast lots: "So Shmuel had all the tribes of Israel come forward and the tribe of Binyamin was taken by lot. He brought the tribe of Binyamin near by its families and the family of Matri was taken by lot. Finally [Shmuel] brought the family of Matri near man by man."[11]

The priest reveals nothing at the time. He says nothing. He allows not even a flicker of emotion to be read in his face. (Most of the younger priests cover their faces with a black veil to prevent the slightest hint of reaction to the casting of the lots from registering.) They have their own means of reckoning these things, our priests. (You, great sage, know a great deal more about such things than I — you who are said to be one of the lights of *gematria*.[12]) Certain letters, in combination, are said to indicate who the sacred couple are. Speculation among some members of the family — never confirmed — suggests that the sum total of letters in King David's name — according to the Hebrew reckoning, fourteen — is the indicator, that this number is a factor in the de-

---

11. 1 Sam. 10:20–21. —FS
12. The cryptographic significance of words. —FS

termination. But my father at least, who knew something about such things, scoffed at that.[13]

In any case, the parents are never told the results of the priests' calculations. Only they know who the Lord has chosen, who the potential mother — called, among us, the "root of the Messiah" — or the father — called "the Messiah's branch" may be.

Obviously, in every generation this is considered a matter of conjecture since it is the Holy One alone who determines the day and the hour when the Messiah will arise. Nevertheless, given the promises made to David, it is our family's unique responsibility to prepare the way for him.

The priests observe the two children from afar, looking for confirming signs, for portents and prophecies. These they gather into a hidden wisdom, a store of stories and maxims, to be discussed only among themselves, which they interpret by means of allegories. As for the children, they are given a normal upbringing.

The priests do not interfere directly in the guidance of the chosen pair, but, naturally, use every means available to them to persuade the lad in question to marry the bride chosen for him, that is, chosen by the priests.

All of which brings me to my own betrothal. It came about this way.

Shortly after my father Jacob's death, the family sent me to Galilee to hide out from political troubles and, in the course of things, to seek out the family of one Miriam, daughter of Joachim, the priest. That was how I came to be in the village of Nazareth. Although Judeans, we had connections in the north country among the towns and villages above the Jezreel Valley, obscure locales where members of our line had been required to hide out from time to time, when Herod the Idumean or his sons began to growl at us. And, as I think you well know, Herod has been doing a great deal more than growling these past years. From his palace in Jericho, sick in mind and body, he has seen fit to send dark winds of terror in every direction like an evil god.

---

13. In Hebrew, as in many ancient languages, the letters of the alphabet are also numbers. This led eventually to a variety of systems of mystical speculation on the meaning of literary texts based on numerical values — in Hebrew *gematria*. For the presence of *gematriot* in the New Testament, see Matthew 1:17: "So all the generations from Abraham to David are fourteen generations; and from David to the deportation to Babylon fourteen generations; and from the deportation to Babylon to the Messiah, fourteen generations." Fourteen is the numerical equivalent of the name "David." —FS

As I've told you, for years we have had to "play the fool" for this usurper, caught as he is between the two lions — the house of David on the one hand, the heirs of the Israelite kingdom, and your Egyptian Ptolemies on the other. (Your Cleopatra, though, used to give the old fox a great more trouble than we, members of the Judean royal family, could ever muster.)

To deflect his well-known rages, we have posed as simple, artless peasants and artisans for a generation. We would appear before him in our sheepskin vests, empty-headed sheepherders without a political instinct in our brains. It used to work. He'd laugh at us and stop speculating for a while about when the house of David might make a grab for the throne. The younger men, in the meantime, would be spirited away to the relative safety of Galilee and wait for things to cool down. In this regard, you must have heard the Judean saying: "The tail of Herod is worse than the head, his second thoughts blacker than the night."

But no more. Do you know what Bethlehemites call Herod these days, after the recent events, after the King of the Jews saw fit to order an attack on Bethlehem itself? Molech, the god who devours children!

But back to the oak tree and my marriage.

I adopted the spot shortly after I came to Nazareth. Always on the lookout for groves of good quality pistachio oak, I was attracted to the site, one of the largest oak forests hereabouts. Making yokes and plows had quickly become my staple employment here, and there's no better raw material for that than this hard, durable wood. But, more than that, I loved the beauty of the great father oak that dominated the grove. It had the look of a sacred tree, like the terebinth for which Herod has constructed a splendid temple at Mamre, where Abraham our father met the three angels and was given the promise of a son.

One day, I hiked out to the hills, heading vaguely in the direction of the old oak. I had a lot on my mind.

It ought to have been so simple. My father, before he died, had urged me — no, ordered — that I seek the hand of Miriam, a distant cousin and daughter of his old friend, Joachim, the priest. While he hadn't said the words as such (the elders never do in our family), I'd understood. Miriam, the daughter of Joachim, was a "chosen" bride. She had lost her parents and was now living with the family of Simon of Clopas in Nazareth.

We'd never met, of course. But I'd known members of the Judean branch of their family and I'd heard things. In fact, I'd long ago assumed from the remarkable tone of respect with which our Jerusalem matrons referred to her that she was considered the family's "prize."

The problem was the Clopas tribe.

Though related to us, and of Davidic heritage, they were the village "n'er-do-wells." It would have been no shame if they had merely been poor. But they were dishonest, too, and, what was worse, insufferably proud. Every other word with them was "the Messiah" — as if to loan them money or to buy their grain was to hasten the day of the Lord.

I kept hesitating. Could it be that my noble father should have wished me to marry into such a viper's brood?

The situation was awkward, as I'm sure you, rabbi, can well appreciate. Should I have made inquiries to Simon, her brother-in-law, I'd have never heard the end of it. He'd have considered the whole thing settled before a sentence was out of my mouth. No, I'd need to determine the thing in my own mind before broaching the topic with the volatile Simon of Clopas.

And as for consulting with one of the priests of our family — that would be to no avail. They never address themselves to such matters directly.

Then one day, in the hills above the village, I saw her. No one needed to say anything to me, no one needed to point her out. I knew instinctively that it was she. Perhaps it was my father's enigmatic description of her, told to me from his sickbed: "Miriam — this one is an ancient child."

(It is as you Alexandrians write about Wisdom: She was as one who had witnessed the creation of Adam and yet was fresher than the dawn.)[14]

She was kneeling in the shadow of the great oak — my oak — gathering wild spices in the shadows. The air was warm and from the large linen bundle at her side one could smell the sage and wild onion, the dill and cumin with which the spring rains had carpeted the soil.

I am sure that it will have occurred to you by now that it was not entirely proper of me to have observed her movements from

---

14. Sir. 24:3. —FS

the bridle path. It is the duty of a pious man to turn his gaze away from the face of woman lest he be led astray by the evil inclination.

But it was the strangest thing, rabbi. Though I determined to resist the impulse to speak to her, I found myself unable to turn my gaze away. Though in appearance like other women, everything about her seemed filled with grace, with an innocence so powerful that it was painful, as though in seeing her, one had plunged one's eyes in a spring of ice-cold water.

It was not desire that rose in me, dear friend, as I gazed at her slow, careful movements beneath the tree. It was fear.

Excursus on the Word "Tektōn"

Carbon copy of note stapled to the back of the translation of Epistle II of the Alexandrian Epistles

No date is given, but internal evidence points to sometime in December 1949. The note was sent to project coordinator Martin Niebel by translator Constantine Gruber.

Okay, good news for the committee, M.N.

Some further points of linkage between our itinerant Egyptian Jewish worker Joseph and the Joseph of the Gospels. And this is hard evidence, mind you, not the sort of textual stuff in the epistles themselves that could well have been interpolated by Christians of later centuries to transform these perfectly innocent documents into a hearty statement of Christian faith. (I admit the parallels between the New Testament and this material are strong, but because the text of the epistles is a crazy-quilt of styles — something not evident from our silken translations — we're not sure where all this stuff comes from or when the document as we now have it was finally stitched together, no doubt by some brilliant, though temporarily unemployed editor — which it surely was.)

You want examples: Well, try this one. Clearly the man Joseph's search for work alone is motive enough to have brought him both to Nazareth and to Egypt. It just so happens that there were huge construction projects going on in those locales during the period that these letters were written, around the time of the death of Herod the Great, in 4 B.C. The messianic mumbo-jumbo allows gods and angels to appear in charge of history rather than the sordid and far less engaging search of an itinerant worker for the means to survive.

Be that as it may, the Joseph described in the Alexandrian Epistles is clearly what we would call today a building contractor. What's interesting for your purposes, my friend, is that that's just what the Joseph of the New Testament is, too.

Sorry to disappoint the faithful, but the Joseph of the Gospels was not — I repeat, not — some sort of father Gepetto figure whittling away at little tables and chairs, all covered with wood shavings.

Joseph is described in the sources as a *tektōn* (Matt. 13:55, Mark 6:3). While there's nothing in the word itself to forbid the performance of carpentry tasks, *tektōn* is more aptly translated "builder."

The word itself in Greek has a wide range of meanings from shipbuilder to mason but generally implies a craftsman of considerable skill. For example, *tektōn can,* depending on the context, be translated "architect." The word can even be used of a physician. Now I'm not implying Joseph was a really a Palestinian neurosurgeon and that what we have in the letters is an exotic medical allegory. But the idea conveyed by the use of the word *tektōn* is someone of remarkable dexterity and professional acumen. If he was a *tektōn,* he was not some poor village wood carver making yokes and plows for the farmers.

He was, in fact, a master craftsman, and master craftsmen in those days were itinerant for the most part, traveling from place to place wherever the work took them. They might travel alone, or they might bring their families with them. Certainly, many of the men of the family and certainly the male offspring of the craftsman would be enlisted as apprentices, often at quite an early age.

So, whoever the bloke is whose experience generated these epistles, the Holy Family of the New Testament was quite definitely Joseph and Son (sons?), Contractors.

In that regard, it must be said that a highland Galilean village like Nazareth would be ideally suited for a *tektōn* because of the opportunity it would offer to settle a family there comfortably close to the key trade and transportation routes. The main cities on the coast, around the Sea of Galilee, and in Samaria could be reached in a day. And we know that in Roman Palestine there was building on a vast scale going on during this period: at Tiberias in Galilee, at Caesarea Maritima on the coast, in Jerusalem, and in Samaria.

Experienced local masters who knew their way around the local building materials — hard woods, limestone, and basalt bricks — they would have been in great demand by the powers that be before the First Roman-Jewish War (A.D. 66).

In like manner, the idea of Joseph as a simple, unlearned tradesman owes more to medieval Europe than to first-century Palestine. For the most part, even eminent rabbis were forbidden to charge for their services as teachers and scholars to the community. They were compelled to earn their living at the various available trades. Learning, wisdom, charismatic leadership juxtaposed with the pursuit of ordinary trades and occupations was common. We have only to think of the example of the second-century Rabbi Akiba, who was a shepherd, or, for that matter, the apostle Paul, who earned his living as a tentmaker (Acts 18:3).

Anyway, dear friend, tell the boys I'm not trying to be difficult. Really, I'm not. And tell Toppler that this memo will cost him — say, fifty Cuban cigars in honor of St. Joseph. All right, ten. And tell him to try not to get more than a few bishops killed this week. It's Christmas. No, on second thought, don't tell him anything, forget the cigars. It will prompt him to visit me.

EPISTLE III

It began, great Jason, as the merest whisper of a rumor, the first small cloud on a clear horizon.

It was a silence at first: an almost imperceptible wariness that seemed to descend on older people when I approached them. Later on, it was looks: the penetrating glance of a Nazareth midwife as she passed me on the village street; a customer, a neighbor of the family of Miriam, my betrothed, who couldn't manage to look me in the face one day when he came to negotiate prices.

Then, like the gradual gathering of storm clouds over the land, it found speech — the simple words of the rural poor who rarely, if ever, say what they really think. "Joseph's bride," they began saying, "grows more radiant by the day."

These words were doubtless repeated dozens of times before I heard them myself one day near the village well.

You, Alexandrian sage, understand, of course, that these rumors did not circulate among us Galileans like they would among Gentiles: for pleasure. No, we Jews cannot, thank God, be accused of that — serving up the misfortunes of our brothers like choice morsels at a feast! It was not with relish that the Nazarenes began to signal each other, sensing the onset of our troubles — Miriam's and mine — but with fear.

Curses, knife fights, brawls have been known to break out over such "incidents" for generations here in the mountain hamlets of Galilee. For example, relations between Nazarenes and the inhabitants of Kefar Cana, the next village, have been tense for decades because, in part, a Nazarene woman was married off to a cousin in Kefar Cana, displacing the interests of a local suitor more than thirty years ago. Their families still fight over the affair. Only last year, two Kefar Cana men were badly beaten up by Nazarenes at a wedding feast when someone starting singing a ditty about it.

"A radiant bride" — however discreet, the meaning of the words was perfectly clear: Joseph's bride bears watching. And should the ensuing weeks bring telltale signs that life already stirred beneath her heart, well....

I struggled with myself for days after the rumors first reached my ears. I could have demanded my right as a fiancé to speak to her, to satisfy myself about her condition in the presence of witnesses. However much a law unto himself, her guardian, Simon, could hardly refuse me that. But I held back. Despite the growing fog of pain that bound up my insides and clouded my mind, I trusted her completely.

Who, knowing her, would have done otherwise? Nazareth women had a reputation for chastity. But she — her purity was something one felt in the very way she breathed. "An ancient child, born before the morning," as my father had said. In her, purity seemed to come, not from some tight internal rein on the passions, or still less from ignorance, but from nature itself — something charming and clean as rain.

Had we all been deceived, then? Had she, a daughter of David, fed on the milk of the Torah, hardy and strong as these hills, allowed herself liberties that would provoke the censure even of pagans?

It was impossible. I had come to that conclusion early on, as I prayed for guidance in the mikveh.[15] (Three times I immersed myself in those purifying waters to seek clarity of vision in this affair: once before proposing the engagement, once during these days of darkness, and, again, when I had come to a decision after the dream.)

This was my determination after prayer: Unless I should hear it from her own lips, I would not allow myself to entertain doubts about her. That duty I firmly placed upon myself. Beyond that, I had known nearly from the start that my fate was bound up with hers in ways that I could not altogether fathom. She was my bride — that was as sure as my name and my craft and the destiny of the sons of David. Whatever happened, whatever humiliations lay hidden, I was determined to be loyal to Miriam, daughter of the priest Joachim.

You will doubtless wish to know the precise reasons for my resolve. You are, after all, a Jew with a Greek education, are you not? (Galileans, as you must have discovered, are not much for "reasons"; we're a people for whom deeds are everything.)

It occurred to me when I first baptized myself in the waters of the mikveh in Sepphoris that the report of Miriam's condition might be a test. You will remember what I told you before about our priests. By means of ordeals, obstacles, loyalty tests they supplemented their mystical calculations with what they called "the tempering of metals." Suppose, I meditated there in the dark waters, that the reports of Miriam's condition were false, spread abroad not by irresponsible people, but at the direction of the council? Suppose this was a trial, a temptation to prove whether my resolve could be weakened by an evil report?

But, O Alexandrian, there was a far deeper and more important reason behind the loyalty I tried to summon in Miriam's regard — a reason you will, I suspect, appreciate more than anyone. Yes, rabbi, the chief reason I took her under my roof has to do with the Logos.

Not that I'd ever heard the word before sitting at your feet in the House of Studies near the Crespus Gate in Alexandria. But years before I had heard the word, I had encountered the reality

---

15. Ritual bath. —CG

of the Logos in the mountains of Galilee, seen it in the face of Miriam.

It occurred to me one starlit night at the door of the synagogue at Sabbath close. We had just been pondering the text that speaks of the angels at Mamre, the angels who announced the promise to Abraham.[16]

One of our number, a visitor who had spent much time among the Gadarenes, wondered aloud if our "messengers" weren't much like the gods of the Greeks who appear occasionally to humans. Our rabbi said simply that, for us Jews, the importance is not what the gods are said to do but what man does, made as he is in the image of God. "Human beings who live the Torah, who live according to the Way of God," he said, "this is the manifestation of heaven, this is the link." Miriam, I suddenly realized, had become just such a link for me. Her every gesture — natural and spontaneous as it seemed — was infused with the beauty, the majesty even, of Torah. Slowly, after our engagement, as my life shaped itself around her, she had become for me not only bride, but the angel of the Torah itself. The rabbi of Nazareth had once said the same thing of her: "The husband of such a woman must be careful. He has the holy scrolls under his roof."

But, O Jason, you can imagine how all that carefully constructed resolve was shaken when the stage of rumor passed and the torment of certainty took its place.

She *was* with child! And this from unimpeachable sources. For my part, I had never allowed myself the liberty of so much as grazing her arm with my sleeve.

(Here it is necessary to add that I have attested this before the council of our family's priests in Bethlehem.)

At the very same time as this news came, other troubles gathered about me. An edict was posted in Sepphoris, the regional capital, to the effect that all male members of the Judean royal line and their families were to report to Bethlehem by a certain date to be officially registered by the authorities. For tax purposes, they said. Anyone not appearing for the census would be fined and — what was worse — prohibited by Roman law from inheriting lands and possessions handed down within the royal family.

---

16. Gen. 18:1–15. —FS

For the family's sake, I knew that I must make the journey south to Bethlehem. Not that it was without its dangers, mind you. The edict bore the unmistakable mark of our mortal enemy, Herod. Gathering the tribe of David together in its ancestral home, ferreting out all the refugees like me who had managed in the past to escape the Idumean's wrath — it was a sensible preparation for a slaughter, we said among ourselves.

With the Romans backing the plan, we had little choice but to show up for our appointed rendezvous with the tax inspectors in Judea. But, already, escape routes were being arranged with the local Bedouin traders should the dying Herod attempt to unsheathe his sword against us one more time.

For me, however, the advancing political storm in Bethlehem was a mere squall in comparison to Nazareth's more intimate whirlwind.

As reports spread about Miriam's condition, a handful of friends, sure of my innocence in the affair, found a convenient target for their anger in Simon of Clopas. (Naturally, at that stage, I'd made no declarations of any kind, not to anyone.) A silence like that of Job the long-suffering enveloped me, almost against my will.

"It's a setup," a contractor in Rakkah ventured. "Clopas has known of the woman's condition for months and has sought to cover her transgression — and line his purse while he's at it — with your good name, Joseph."

"Thou shalt not kill, Amnon," I told him, referring to the principle that an evil report, even if true, wounds as surely as a knife.

But it did occur to me one day that, perhaps — God forbid! — Miriam might have been attacked by some Roman soldier on the bridle path above the town. It had happened before to one village girl some five years earlier. (And Clopas's business relations with the Roman garrison in Sepphoris were known to be cozy.)

But such reasoning stirred only the surface of the waters, O sage. What I am about to tell you now is what I found in the depths of the experience, what I found in the darkness of the mikveh when I prayed there the second time. Do not dismiss what I have written here through Simon the scribe. Take it, if you must, as a record of the workings of one mind coming to a decision.

Sure that some hidden fault had hurled me into this abyss of shame, I immersed myself seven times in the waters. "Cleanse me, O God, of hidden faults," I prayed again and again.[17] There, in the dark waters, the name of my betrothed came to mind: Miriam, sister of *Moshe Rabbeinu,* Moses our teacher, the singer of victory at the edge of the sea.

As it is written: "The prophetess Miriam, Aaron's sister, took a tambourine in her hand, while all the women went out after her with tambourines, dancing; and she led them in the refrain: 'Sing to the Lord, for he is gloriously triumphant; horse and chariot he has cast into the sea....' "[18]

(It is wise always to believe what one hears in the depths of repentance, when pride has been cast aside and the ear opened to life.)

There also I remembered the meaning of the name of my betrothed: the water that is sweet and bitter. (I recall that you told me once that the name, in Egyptian, means "beloved of God.")

When I went below the surface of the water for the seventh time, the passage entered my mind: "And a branch shall sprout from the stump of Jesse, and from his root, a bud shall blossom...."[19]

I came up trembling.

How could I have been so long in seeing it, I pondered? How could I — credited with the best contractor's eye in Galilee — miss what had been before my eyes from the beginning — the "other" explanation for the events?

The various "reasonable" scenarios had long since ceased to interest me, in any case. They all failed to account for the one central fact, the one on which I would have staked my life: Miriam's unassailable innocence. Could it be that there was some more mysterious purpose at work here than the mechanics of a sordid rural tragedy?

Could Miriam be the "root" — the one through whom Messiah would come? The words formed themselves in my mind like a solution to a puzzle. All my life had been lived in the shadow of that precise possibility. No, I had not gone mad. Had I a better explanation of the events of the past weeks? In a thousand years, no

---

17. Ps. 19:12. —FS
18. Exod. 15:20–21. —FS
19. Isa. 11:1. —FS

"chosen bride" of our family had conducted herself dishonorably. It was unthinkable.

These are strange matters. In our family, it's told that Bathsheba was one of the king's "chosen brides," chosen by God to bear Solomon the Wise, but betrothed instead to a foreign mercenary. Through complex mystical paths — we call them the "paths of shame" — she was joined, our family elders say, to her true husband and her destiny.

I began to weep. Weeks of strain and uncertainty poured themselves out in the darkness. And also sadness. For, in that moment, I knew that I would never be the husband of the daughter of Joachim, the priest. If God had selected Miriam as the "root of the Messiah," could there be any doubt that he would find a more worthy spouse for this treasure than a highland tradesman — a man who was not even a scholar?

I must free her at once, I determined, of any obligation to me. Miriam must be free, at all costs.

Managing to preserve some semblance of the niceties of procedure, I sent a message to Miriam's guardian, requesting an interview with my bride before the next Sabbath.

The whole situation grew more complicated by the hour.

The council in Cana had already summoned me for a discreet session on the evening after Shabbat. I had no choice but to appear before them, to take or deny responsibility for the conception of the child. If I were to admit paternity — that I had "soiled my own bed," as the saying went, "that I had eaten my grapes unripened," as the Galilean women sing — no great harm done, all told. I would have to pay Clopas a fine and could never divorce the bride I'd apparently defiled.

People, of course, would feel free to be disappointed in a man once thought so marriageable — a "royal one." Local rabbis would not often call me forward to read from the Torah portion for the Sabbath. My sons and daughters would not be welcome to marry into the more socially prominent families of Sepphoris or Cana.

But if I told the truth, that I had not touched the lovely daughter of Joachim, I would, in the words of the Law, "expose her." And while the few rabbis who serve these villages are able enough to devise a charitable solution to such things, there's no telling what a Galilean mob might do should she show her face in the town.

They stoned a woman in a village by the lake last year before the council fathers could spirit her away.

The old people hereabouts say that unchaste deeds "poison the air." They make for barren wombs, diseased livestock, and unproductive fields.

Finally, numb inside, I made my way one evening, as pre-arranged, to the house of Simon of Clopas on the slope at the village edge, into an inner chamber where Miriam lay resting. Simon himself stood there in the doorway, motionless, like a man vanquished by something he cannot begin to understand.

As my eyes fell on her for the first time in weeks, I could confirm the verdict of others: Indeed, she was with child; and indeed, she was more radiant than I had ever seen her before.

Our eyes met briefly. For me, everything hung upon the reading of that look, like the soundings sailors take to keep them from perilous shallows.

What would I find there?

To my surprise, I found in her face a look of such luminous vindication that I had to turn from it. It was as if she were the barren Sarah triumphant with Isaac or the fallen Bathsheba carrying the heir in her womb.

My knees grew weak, sending my body slumping to the stone floor facing her. Great sage, this poor man hadn't the slightest idea what course of action to pursue now. Not even the questions to ask the wondrous creature before me.

It was she who broke the silence that had enveloped the two of us, the room, the house, the earth.

"Don't be afraid," she said as she took my hand and laid it on the place where the child grew.

Excursus on Ritual Baths
by Constantine Gruber

A typewritten half-page is inserted here in the translation. It is on poor-quality wartime paper stock, the blue-lined sort used in primary schools.

Julia:

Please type this up on better paper — if you can find some. Remind Martin that we're in need of a tad more generosity

from the committee when it comes to basic supplies. Tell him
to burgle a school or something. But tell him nicely.

STANZ

In Epistle III, Joseph bathes twice in a mikveh, or ritual bath,
for purification and, specifically, for wisdom about the dilemma of
his marriage. The practice has its antecedents in ancient Israelite
practice and also in the various religious traditions of the pagan
world. Bathing for ritual or spiritual reasons clearly prepares the
way for the central Christian rite of baptism.

Ancient Israelite tradition prescribed ritual bathing for the removal of certain impediments to worship: for example, one must
bathe after being cured of leprosy (Lev. 15:11–27) and after
touching a corpse (Num. 19:19).

The Book of Kings tells the story of Naaman, the Syrian's cure
from leprosy by "immersing himself seven times in the Jordan
[River]" (2 Kings 5:14) and the Old Testament Deuterocanonical
book of Judith describes the heroine immersing herself repeatedly
in a spring in order to purify herself for the slaying of the Assyr-
ian general Holofernes — that is, before a redemptive deed that
involves the taking of a life (Judith 12:7).

Early Judaism also knew the practice of baptizing proselytes, or
Gentiles who had joined the synagogue.

In this connection, it is worth noting that the mystery religions
of the pagan world were "baptism"-oriented as well. The devotee
descended into the bath in order to be ritually cleansed and also
to receive a token of immortality. In the rite, the adept symboli-
cally dies ("drowns") and is raised to new life. The notion seems
to come from Egypt, where the belief was common that to drown
in the Nile was to become divinized.

The Jewish historian Josephus indicates that by the Second
Temple period, ritual ablutions of various sorts and for various
purposes were widely practiced. Jewish sects like the Essenes regularly performed ritual washings and not only, apparently, for the
removal of purely ritual impediments, but also as an aid to interior
reform.

Clearly the Joseph of the epistles approaches the mikveh, or ritual bath, with this in mind. He specifically mentions going down
into the water seven times and even appears to regard this sort of
immersion — at least potentially — as an occasion for revelation.

We ought to visualize such mikvaot, or ritual baths, as covered cisterns dug out next to or near synagogues or, in the case of Jerusalem, as surrounding the Temple enclosure.

There the devotees would descend stairs cut out of the rock and, doffing their clothes, would immerse themselves in the pool while an attendant of the same sex stood by to insure that the ritual was properly performed. (Normally, men and women used separate facilities.)

Jesus' cousin John the Baptist (or, better, Baptizer) made a virtual career out of administering a "repentance baptism," chiefly in rivers (Mark 1:4, Matt. 3:1, Josephus: *Antiquities* 18:5.2), an activity in which Jesus himself engaged, albeit indirectly, through his disciples (John 3:22, 4:2).

EPISTLE IV

What man, save you, Jason, sage of Egypt, has the knowledge of so many hidden things? It is partly, of course, for that reason that I trust you with these confidences, these wonders that I have touched with my own unworthy hands. Most men, however learned, upon reading what I have written to you would surely shake their hands and think me the victim of some desert fever or, worse, a man whom love or shame had driven mad.

Others — fervent souls, like the excitable chiefs of the Gaza synagogue, looking for messiahs under the flap of every tent — would, on hearing my tale, crown me King of Israel on the spot!

No, it is not the breadth of your experience alone that allows me to trust you, great one: but the breadth of your embrace. Does not the Song of Songs read:

> "His left hand is under my head
> and his right arm embraces me"?[20]

Well, you, sage, embrace all your sons with both arms: the hand of your prudence under our heads and with the right arm, compassion, you envelop us. Half the refugees of Alexandria have you for a father. And all her seekers.

---

20. Song 8:3. —FS

With that in mind, attend then to the most difficult, the most wondrous part of my tale.

༜

Did you not tell me once, friend of my soul, that when Antony the Roman still ruled Alexandria, on the day before he died at Cleopatra's feet, you heard with your own ears the strange heavenly music of his gods? The story now is widely known how the whole city on that night of destiny was blanketed with the sounds of a heavenly troupe, the sound of Antony's demons abandoning him to his fate. You told me one crisp Alexandria night that you yourself, then a mere boy, unable to sleep because of the awful stillness, had heard it: the heavenly music.

This will make it easier for you, then, to understand my own fateful night in Bethlehem nearly three years ago when I too heard music from the skies.

It was so still that night on the top of the ridge as I stood guard outside the cave. The heavens were alive with lights — no, not only stars, but strange veils shimmering with color that would descend out of the blackness as though the great star-studded curtain of the Temple itself were being torn. It was the stillness not of contentment, but of anticipation.

Miriam was settled within, in the heart of the cave, warmed by the heat of an earthen oven stoked with hot coals. She was sure it would be tonight. Quite certain. And I had learned not to question her.

I was not alone on my watch. Because of the census, the whole city was crammed with people, filling inns and roof tops, lining streets and now scavenging the caves at the city's edge for shelter. Those latecomers who hadn't managed to make it to the city by sunset when the gates were sealed for the night had had to arrange matters for themselves with the Bedouin traders who were nearly always encamped nearby, ever ready to offer space in their capacious tents for high fees — higher according to the level of fear they read in the eyes of potential customers. After all, packs of jackals and wild dogs were not uncommon night visitors to Bethlehem's gates, looking for animal carcasses.

Even people within the town were on edge. What was the real purpose, people wondered, behind this crazy census of the Davidic line, administered by Romans but no less clearly designed by Herod? Why couldn't we have just registered in our own towns and villages, people asked, rather than to have to journey all the way here — and at such expense — to Bethlehem?

But there were more ominous aspects to the affair and, more than the mere inconvenience, it was these that were making people jittery. Perhaps it's a trap, people worried. In the past, the madman wouldn't have dared. But everyone knew he was at death's door. What if old Herod, stewing in his steam bath, had hatched this whole census scheme in order to round off his bloody reign with a politically convenient massacre of Bethlehem's brightest and best?

That was why the city fathers had paid the Bedouin handsomely to be on hand for the census. They might well be marauders, these tribes from beyond the Jordan, but they were also incomparable spies. Beyond that, at least a few of the leading families could be hidden away among their caravans in a crisis.

But my mind was not fixed on the census or on what Herod might be up to. For months now, I had found that I only lived for one thing, for them — for my bride and the child. Each day the devotion grew broader, occupying yet another faculty, like an underground spring wending its way through the rock.

You must try to understand me, rabbi.

From my boyhood, I had sought to be a son of the Torah. I kept the commandments, not out of fear, but because each of the mitzvot — even the smallest — seemed to me to shimmer with holy fire. If only the scales could fall from my eyes, I knew that even the smallest, most apparently insignificant precept was a mirror held up to the very face of God.

But, as a Galilean, I was never content merely to sit in the House of Studies with my head in a scroll, blocking out the great world outside with the hum of study. All my days, then and now, were spent out under the skies handling the things of the earth — wood and stone and pigment and tar. With my ancestor David, I cried out: "Lord, open my eyes that I may see wonders out of your Torah!"[21]

And I did see. The more diligently I studied Torah, the more clearly I discovered God's presence not merely in the commentaries of the rabbis or the few poorly maintained scrolls over which I'd pored, but in the simple glories of the Galilee and in the business of daily life.

---

21. Ps. 119:18. —FS

I know, sage, that you are smiling as you read this. You Alexandrians are specialists in the notion that the Torah is not merely a text, however holy, but a presence in the universe.

But long before I sat with your disciples in the House of Studies near the Crespus Gate, I'd seen it. I'd encountered the beauty of Torah in a person.

Yes, that day under the great oak, when I first saw Miriam, the daughter of Joachim, gathering spices. It was what had so moved me on that occasion. The same beauty, the same truth I'd discovered in the cadences of the Psalms or in the dazzle of the sky on Mount Tabor or in seeing an injustice righted or a poor man's bitterness relieved — all that was in her.

In the months that followed our engagement, that perception became sharper. Her every attitude, her innocence and wisdom, her candor, the strange quick wince of pain that would cross her face if she chanced upon some misdeed, her subtle, shy humor — it was indeed as if a kind of spiritual pinnacle had been reached in this simple daughter of Israel, as if Torah had created a dwelling place for itself in her.

Now I'm not a learned man, but I know enough to realize what I have written amounts to walking on sand: any moment such speculations may cause a man to sink forever out of sight, "swallowed" — the phrase is a Jerusalemite one — "by philosophy."

But you Alexandrians are bold enough for such things, aren't you? Do you yourself, rabbi, not teach that Lady Wisdom "is an aura of the might of God and a pure effusion of His glory . . . a spotless mirror of the working of God, and an image of his goodness"?

"I loved her and sought her from my youth," sang Solomon,
"I desired to take her for my bride,
and became enamored of her beauty. . . . "[22]

But I'd promised to tell you about the music, hadn't I?

It was shortly after the Roman watch was changed, when the night had run its course and we begin to calculate the dawn that I heard the music. At first, it was like the soft jangle of glass beads in a gentle wind. Then there was a thundering, like an earthquake at first, and then like the hooves of a thousand horses hurtling

---

22. Wisd. 7:25–26; 8:2. —FS

down a valley. The racket of invisible wheels creaked on the wind, to be followed by a bray that was like the sound of numberless horns. Then a long chord sounded — one feared it would go on forever, one prayed it would never cease — a fan of music that transformed itself in infinite variety across the whole range of registers. It wound itself at last into the moan of a strong, driving gale sweeping over the cloudless sky. And with a cascade of tinkling glass, it was gone.

The strange display so astonished me that it took me some moments to realize that another, smaller, sound — a sharp cry — had begun to pierce the darkness behind me.

EPISTLE V

We parted at the place of the three roads, at the foot of Bethlehem's hill, where the steep path to David's city meets the ribbon of road south to Hebron. The sky was dark, moonless. That, at least, was fortuitous. With their unwieldy entourage of servants, pack animals, and wagons, the sages needed all the help the elements could provide for their lumbering escape from Herod's swift and sleepless wrath.

The mysterious sages who came by night to examine the Child! Doubtless, O Jason, you have had an earful from the traders and the others about that episode by now.

But surely you, an Alexandrian, understand better than most how many such seers populate our part of the world: awash in lore about the birth of heroes and the meaning of the stars.

It's not that I'm cynical about such things. Who would not be intrigued by the sight of the "lights" of Mesopotamia encamped in all their finery outside his door?

But, for myself, I had no need of Babylonian magi to confirm the wonder of my son Joshua's birth. Their star maps, their expert readings of sheep livers, their incense-inspired prophecies added nothing to what I already knew.

I had only to peer into my son's child-eyes to know more than any diviner could ever tell me about his destiny. Even you, rabbi, have spoken to me about it on several occasions. What were the words you used? "He looks both astonished and sad at the same time." Yes, that almost captures it: Even from his earliest infancy, the clarity of those eyes was enough to make one turn away, that gaze of wonder and agony.

But the thing that troubled me most about the magi had little to do with their divinations. It was the publicity they brought with them. After all, my chief concern at this point was to return with my family to Nazareth as quickly and as discreetly as possible. Reports indicated that tempers there had cooled. And, in any case, it was safer to be taking one's chances with compatriots in Galilee than to sit here in Bethlehem like a target.

Unwittingly, the Babylonians had put Herod on our trail — Herod whose rages against real and perceived opponents had reached epic proportions. Had the madman not weeks before imprisoned his own son, the heir Antipater, on a trumped-up charge? What might the tyrant dream up for a Davidic usurper on his doorstep?

I could not help but notice that even the inscrutable Bedouin were jumpy as they escorted the Babylonians onto the Hebron road. Try as they might to avoid alerting Roman patrols ahead, the rumble of their heavy wagons could be heard for miles.

We parted at the place of the three roads, where the paths form a Roman cross. As a host, I'd felt it my duty to accompany the eminent guests that far, to the end of Bethlehem land at least. But as the caravan prepared to veer south, the chief sage approached me suddenly in the darkness. Bowing low, without a word, he pressed something into my hand. It was cold, like a lump of glass. Then, looking me straight in the face, he said just one word: "Flee."

✤

At first, even in the warm glow of burning lamps, I couldn't make out what I held in my hand, what the sage had given me. A talisman of some sort I supposed. Then, bringing a clay lamp close by, I realized that it was a large, uncut ruby that lay cupped in my palm.

The stone shimmered in the light like Passover wine.

"Flee." The word resounded again. But where? No such treasure would be required for the trek back north to Galilee. Bread and water, some vegetables, feed for the pack animals — no more than a week's wages was needed to do that. Rubies however were the preferred method of payment for the hard passage across the desert. It enabled the Bedouin caravan drivers to enhance their earnings by bartering in Alexandria or in the resort cities of the

Delta. And what could that mean other than Egypt, the traditional haven of Jews fleeing disaster?

I washed my hands and sat down on one of the stone benches facing the inner chamber where the tomb of *Rachel Imanu* — Rachel our mother — lay covered in dark, gold-embroidered cloth. As you remember, beloved sage, her tomb has always had an honored place among us at the place of the three roads, where the Torah tells us she died giving birth to Benjamin, youngest son of the patriarch Jacob.

Every Bethlehemite knows the text by heart: "And when they were still some distance from Ephrath, Rachel travailed, and she had hard labor. And when she was in her hard labor, the midwife said to her, 'Fear not; for now you will have another son.' And as her soul was departing (for she died), she called her son Benoni — that is, 'son of my sorrow.' ... So Rachel died and she was buried on the way to Ephrath (that is, Bethlehem), and Jacob set up a pillar on her grave; it is the pillar of Rachel's tomb, which is there to this day."[23]

I knew the place well. When a boy, I'd often hide from my cousins here, concealing myself behind the Matriarch's cenotaph. And later, forced by circumstances to seek refuge in Galilee, I'd taken comfort from the old saying that Rachel Our Mother lies buried beside the Hebron road in order to weep for her children who must pass that way in exile.

> "Thus says the Lord: A voice is heard in Ramah,
> lamentation and bitter weeping.
> Rachel is weeping for her children;
> and she refuses to be consoled ... "[24]

It is said by locals that should one fall asleep by Rachel's grave, one may hear in slumber a voice arising from the deeps, answering one's deepest prayers. My namesake, Joseph, on his way to slavery in Egypt, once heard that voice, it is said. His captors, encamped at Ephrath near the tomb, allowed the poor lad to grieve there.

"Arise, see your son, and weep with me over my misfortune," he is said to have prayed. Asleep against his mother's grave, he heard her voice prophesying all that would later happen to him.

---

23. Gen. 35:16–20. —FS
24. Jer. 31:15 —FS

That night, the stone tomb blazed with light. The married women of Bethlehem had come there only that afternoon to tie red ribbons about the monument, as is their custom, and pray for fertility and a safe delivery at the Matriarch's tomb.

As for me, I'd come here to think, to get my mental bearings before climbing the steep path back up to Bethlehem and a family that, rightly, expected decisions to be made.

We had little time to lose. Within hours, Roman patrols would have informed Herod of the sages' treachery. Retaliation would be swift.

The parameters of the decision were clear: A three-day trek to Nazareth, where there was family, where one was known, where every inch of the terrain was familiarity itself; or a perilous two-week hike across the Sinai to exile in the land of Egypt where, at best, a stranger's life awaited.

Egypt: It would be madness to seek refuge there.

❧

I must have fallen asleep there in the warm lamp-lit room before the cenotaph of Rachel. The next thing I remember is the voice of high winds outside, the whoosh of the branches of the cypress trees that ringed the low-domed building.

"Arise, my son," ... The words rang in my ears.

I must be going, I started, sitting up. God knows how long I have been dozing here. Miriam will begin to worry.

It wasn't until I'd stepped into the now frigid night air, however, that I realized that my mind was astonishingly clear.

All the previous confusion and irresolution were gone. It was like a fever breaking in the sweat of sleep.

The steep ascent to the city lay before me in the darkness, bereft of travelers. That was as it should be, I said to myself. Respectable people had long since bolted their doors against the night's multiple unknowns.

But on closer inspection, I was not alone at the fork of the three roads.

It took a few moments for my eyes to focus on the figure standing silent and motionless in the middle of the roadway. Late arrival, pilgrim, brigand, spy? But a few steps closer and I observed that, although his face was still hidden, he wore the mantle of our family's priests. I breathed a sigh of relief. A messenger from the council, no doubt, sent by Miriam to fetch me.

"Shalom," I said warmly.

"Hurry, Joseph," the man rasped, taking my arm, "take the child and his mother, flee to Egypt, and stay there until I tell you."[25]

"You are the council's angel?" I asked.

"Yes, yes. Hurry. The Bedouin are waiting to escort you. Herod moves against us tonight."

I felt in the pocket of my caftan for the ruby. It was still there, buried beneath the roots of my fingers — the last gift of the magi.

Excursus on the Flight into Egypt
by Friedrich Schleyer

Based on the New Testament account of the flight into Egypt (Matt. 2:13–15), Coptic, or traditional Egyptian Christianity has set apart literally dozens of sites throughout the Nile Delta and Middle Egypt in honor of their journey. Many of these reflect local tradition and folklore rather than historical probability.

For example, Christians and Muslims alike celebrate the annual pilgrimage to Gebel al-Tair (the Mountain of Birds) in Middle Egypt where, according to Egyptian tradition, Jesus left his childish imprint on a boulder that was about to topple on him.

Quite naturally, the shrine church built at the site, called Our Lady of Palms, is venerated as a place of healing.

A reader familiar with Egyptian history would also note the thematic similarities between the concerns of the tale of Gebel al-Tair with those of the older Isis-Osiris tradition in which the Great Mother of Egypt hid her son from those who sought to harm him.

While there are significant differences in detail between Christian and Muslim traditions about the route the Holy Family would have traveled, the main outlines of the itinerary are well-established in Egyptian lore. Among the places where the Holy Family is said to have rested on their journey are the towns of Tel Basta, Bilbais, Samanud, and Sakha in the Delta; also the area of Wadi Natrun west of the delta, which plays host to one of Egypt's principal monastic centers. Old Cairo can boast a site or two and nearby Heliopolis enjoys popularity as the place where the Virgin refreshed herself beneath a balsam tree and washed the clothes of

---

25. See Matt. 2:13. —FS

the Christ child in the spring. Today's "tree of the Virgin" grew from the shoot of a sycamore planted in 1672.[26] The village of Maadi[27] claims a set of rock stairs to the Nile from which the Holy Family embarked on its river journey to Upper Egypt.

The banks of the Nile are studded with sites associated with this epic sojourn: at Bahnasa, Kais, Gebel al-Tair, Ashmounein, Phyls, and, according to Coptic (not Muslim) sources, Assiyut, where, it is said, the Holy Family resided in rock tombs in the mountains. The traditions unite, however, around the notion that the holy travelers journeyed southwest from Qusia to Meir and el-Muharrak. There Joseph built a modest house out of bricks and covered it with palm leaves. And, according to tradition, it was at el-Muharrak that the angel appeared to Joseph and informed him that he could return to the land of Israel (Matt. 2:20).

Beyond the mythological elements in the story and its parallels with the themes of earlier Pharaonic belief, particularly the cult of Isis, there is, in fact, a historical substratum to the Egyptian account of the flight into Egypt. And that historical bedrock rests on the parallels between the sites associated with the Holy Family in Coptic and Muslim tradition and the location of the worker camps and outposts along the Nile during the Augustan age.

Is there something more here than each region of the country wishing its portion of the head of Osiris? It would appear so, but, obviously, much further research will have to be done along these lines to say for sure.[28]

EPISTLE VI

This, Jason, God's dove among the Gentiles, is the last of the missives I, Joseph, your son, leave to your care.

Tomorrow, our peril having passed, we set out for the Land of Israel once more.

Yes, sage, the angel of the council, the messenger I encountered three years ago at the place of the three roads outside Bethle-

---

26. Sadly, it fell on June 14, 1906. —CG
27. Now a suburb of Cairo. —CG
28. But see my "The Journey of the Holy Family in Egypt and Ancient Worker Colonies in the Fayoum: Notes toward a Thesis" in *Journal of Coptic Studies*, London, April 1949. —CG

hem appeared one night at the door to the workman's shelter at Pelusium in the Fayoum, asking for me.

He showed me the Bethlehem star, which is the special insignia of our priests, and recited the directions given him: "Rise," he said, "take the child and his mother and return to the Land of Israel. Those who sought the child's life are dead."[29]

As before, his visit was preceded by nights of strange dreams — dreams by day and by night. In the night, there's a pure blue opening in a cloud-framed sky penetrated by flocks of wild geese rising on the winds in pursuit of an eagle. By day, all the sounds of the earth seem louder and deeper than usual, and Galilee birds I have never once seen in the Fayoum — white cranes and kingfishers — buzz past me on the paths to the stone quarry.

And I can always tell when some new development's about to dawn from watching Miriam. Normally her movements as she works are neither quick nor slow, but careful, patient, and focused as if the task at hand were the only thing in the world.

But when changes are in the wind, a touch of restlessness and distractedness comes over her.

The angel stayed with us another day, enjoying the spring cucumbers and fava beans Miriam had planted, and telling us all the news.

Herod the Great, dead these past three months, can, it seems, trouble us no longer. The common opinion is that Prince Archelaus, the heir, is a nearly toothless lion. The Romans, having turned a blind eye all these years to the father's crimes — with terrible results — have little cause to similarly coddle the son.

What a wretched death he died, Herod — the man who drowned innocence in blood on Bethlehem's streets.

On hearing the news, our whole family fell quiet, stunned, hardly able to take it all in — the sheer scale of the man's life, his accomplishments, his rages, his end.

As for me, I felt as if a Roman cross had been lifted from my shoulders. Not that Egypt hasn't been generous to me, my friend. But does not the Psalm say: "I had rather a day in your courts than a thousand elsewhere; I had rather lie at the threshold of the house of my God than dwell in the tents of the wicked"?[30]

---

29. See Matt. 2:19–20. —FS
30. Ps. 84:10. —FS

Miriam said something similar a few days ago after we heard the news about Herod. She came to me with light shining in her eyes: "Did you hear what was read from Hosea, the prophet, in the synagogue on the Sabbath, how the prophet said, 'When Israel was a child I loved him, and out of Egypt, I have called my son'?"[31]

This is not to say, dear friend, that we haven't considered your advice sent to us by way of the merchant Demetrius: to wait, to take stock of all the new political developments before we act. Still, given everything, we will take your advice as proof of your love and take our chances on holy soil. After all, now that the angels have uncrossed their swords from the gates of our paradise, it's best not to linger long, I think.

And so tomorrow we leave Egypt.

Strange, though, how on this shining night of freedom, I'm reminded of the day when we made our way into exile.

❧

It was firstlight in Gaza, gate of the Sinai, three years ago. The moon, still visible, hovered like a great bird over the endless bluegreen sea of desert.

The day we left for Alexandria, I had finally managed to dredge up a minyan[32] from among the refugees. "*Shacharit* — morning service," I'd whispered for the third day in a row against the tent flaps of those, like me, awaiting passage across the sand.

Amid groans and the traders' vivid curses, today, at long last, ten souls stumbled out of their slumber long enough to join me in chanting the psalms, readings, and blessings enjoined on us by our forefathers.

"Blessed are you, O Lord our God, King of the Universe," we murmured, facing Jerusalem, "for not making me a slave. Blessed are you, O Lord our God, King of the Universe, for not making me a heathen."

The words flowed over me like olive oil on wounds. Such words, such rituals would, so it seemed, be our sole possession in exile, the shield that would prevent our being crushed by the poverty and restlessness of a stranger's life.

Behind us, a few yards away as we prayed, was the border —

---

31. Hos. 11:1 —FS
32. The required quorum of Israelites for prayer. —FS

for us Jews the greatest single frontier in the universe: the border between the Land of Israel and the nations.

As you, O sage, recall, that's a distinction every Jewish schoolboy knows. "What are the ten degrees of holiness?" I can still hear the old Bethlehem rabbi's husky voice as he drilled us in the synagogue. The holiest place in the world is the Holy of Holies in the Temple where God's presence dwells. Then follow the seven other sites in the Temple. Then Jerusalem, the Holy City, which surrounds it, and, finally, the Land of Israel itself, the tenth degree of holiness.

Beyond was not, simply, the rest of the world, but lands of darkness and dispersion.

Do not Jews returning from exile shake the dust of the nations off their sandals before setting foot on holy ground again?

"Blessed are you, O Lord our God, King of the Universe," the pilgrims pray, "who has sustained us in life and allowed us to enter the realms of holiness."

There's no blessing for passing over into the realm of the nations — what the mystics call *Sitra Achra* — the "Other Side": the place of temptation and infidelity, of unclean foods and forbidden deeds, of cultures under the dark sway of demons, their peoples given over to futility, to the worship of idols.

As we finished the *Amidah,* the prayer said standing, fishermen were already spreading their nets on the Gaza shore and the caravan drivers had begun to bridle the pack animals for the long day's journey.

In just a few hours, our caravan, manned by the Arab traders whose expertise consisted in forging paths across the trackless dunes, would lumber across that great invisible boundary. Despite the solace that the singing of the Morning Service had provided, I had to admit that I was afraid. Afraid and worried. About the journey and its uncertainties, yes. But mostly about Miriam.

It took a day or two for news of the Bethlehem massacre to filter into Gaza. The Kedarites had more or less abandoned us at a refugee encampment near the sea where one could vie for days for space on one of the twice-weekly caravans to Alexandria.

Both Miriam and I had foreseen that Herod's soldiers might well loot Bethlehem in the course of searching for the child. But we'd hoped that our flight might forestall the worst. Miriam took the news of the death of the children very hard.

At first she was silent. Then she refused all food. I knew better than to try to reason with her and accepted the situation as best I could. For days, it seemed as though the only sound I could hear was my own breathing.

And then one afternoon when I'd come back to our tent from yet another fruitless attempt to secure space on the next junket, I found her sitting inside with her hair uncovered and the sleeves of her tunic torn at the seams, as one does at the death of a relative.

The child was nestled in her lap, awake. As I sat down myself, wordlessly, in a corner, I observed that both child and mother had the same expression in their eyes: a gaze like that of an animal, full of pain and wonder.

In the unity of the mother and child, it seemed as though Miriam and Joshua had become only one person, as though by rending her garments, Miriam were acting out the child's wishes.

I shuddered. It came to me then as words; before it had only been a feeling. These two — this mother and child — were utterly without guile, even the guile of self-interest. They were utterly unprotected in this world. Even the youngest children weave skins of self-preservation, cultivate habits through which to fend off the perils of the world. But not these two. Theirs was the terrible innocence of God.

Finally, as if sensing my discomfort, Miriam looked up at me and, letting out a deep sigh, said only, "Blessed be God, the true judge...."

"Amen," I replied...

"...who vindicates the faith of martyrs," she added, pulling her veil over her head before beginning preparations for the evening meal.

☙

All this comes back to me now, Jason, as I stand once more on the threshold of the desert, on the threshold of my strange destiny. Not, of course, that I'm the same person I was three years ago — thanks to you, rabbi. Yes, old friend, in parting, I feel it a special duty to tell you how much I treasure all your teachings. Above all, the very first thing you taught me: about the meaning of exile.

You remember, of course, how fearful I was when we first arrived in Alexandria — not of the practical challenges we faced so much as the spiritual ones: the challenge of living in the land of dispersion, of life outside the borders of Israel. Surely you recall our many late-night discussions in the synagogue courtyard on that topic — my endless questions.

But it was you, Jason, who taught me by the very holiness that is yours, that "holy land" can be anywhere, anywhere where God's will is performed. There, in that place, in that house, be it the corner of a room where a poor one cries out to God, there he may be rightly said to rule. Where men accept the Torah, indeed where they struggle with it as our father Jacob struggled with the angel at the River Jabbok, there the holy Presence rests.

But where wickedness and rejection thrive — though it be in the shadow of the Temple itself — can the Dove of God be there? One might as well shake its dust from one's shoes as one does when leaving a pagan land.

Well, Jason, light of Alexandria, I take my leave of you with tears. *Shalom uvracha* — peace and a blessing.

I have told you all I know about the mysteries of the child's birth. The rest remains hidden in the heart of God. Do not trouble yourself about these matters, though, great sage. Let them nest in your bosom, father of Egypt, until the day when they take wing all by themselves.

JOSEPH

[by the hand of the Simon the mute, scribe of Pelusium, who makes his mark here]

Chapter 3

The Sons of Joseph

Notebooks on the Mar Yusuf Community
by Friedrich Schleyer and Constantine Gruber

Editor's Note

No, dear reader, despite the title of this chapter, the multiple purveyors of this modest library are not now about to take you on a tantalizing tour of the much-vexed historical question of the "brothers and sisters" of Jesus. We feel sure that the audience for such a work as this will be more than familiar with the problem: namely, in what sense the four men (James, Joseph, Simon, and Judas) and women (names and number unspecified) listed in Matthew 13:55–56 as brothers and sisters of Jesus of Nazareth are to be considered siblings. Curiously, for a work deriving, ostensibly, from the family of Christ, the Joseph Archive is as indecisive as the Gospels themselves appear to be on this point.

No, the "sons of Joseph" to which this material alludes are the monks of the Egyptian monastic community of Mar Yusuf who referred to themselves in this manner, at least according to a few ribbons of text found in the margins of the Joseph Archive that may be safely ascribed to them.

As in the Joseph Archive itself, this is a drama of adoptive, not blood, relations.

The notebooks that follow function as a sizeable excursus on the ancient monastic community that, depending on the reader's point of view, produced or handed down these texts ascribed to Joseph the Builder — or both.

Unfortunately, despite the efforts of our researchers, we cannot add any new information to what is written here about the monastery — not even so much as a scrap or two of confirmatory evidence that the monastery ever existed. Surely, the reader says to himself, a short visit to the Fayoum would have settled that question. Exactly. In fact, most of the mysteries encountered in these pages could be dispelled in a matter of weeks by a first-rate, properly financed effort. But research here at the Review has never been adequately funded. Travel for the most part has always been out of the question. And when we fell afoul of the old regime, well....

Is it vulgar for us to hope that our earnest underfunded efforts on the Joseph Archive might, after all, persuade a few research grants in our direction? We are amazed to read of the vast sums Americans spend each year bottling the air of graves, on reassembling shards of undistinguished colonial period china shattered *in situ* by drunk drivers with an insufficient awareness of the necessity of municipal museums on their way to oblivion.

Be that as it may, what follows is what can only be called a collage of historical notes from various periods put into shape — if "shape" is the word we want — by the translator Constantine Gruber, probably in early 1950. —Ed.

Excerpts from documents generated during the second forgery hearing of Doctor Friedrich Schleyer of the University of Leipzig on charges filed by the trustees of the Department of Antiquities, University of Breslau, May 6–8, 1878, in the Prussian State Court building, Breslau

Case No. 33991 (a)
Records, Vol. 14, transcript 909, pp. 23–39

1. **Affidavit #1, Sent by Maximillian Eastman, Director of Field Work, Coptic Museum, Alexandria, April 4, 1878.**

[*Note:* Eastman explains to the president of the court, Dr. Klaus Schwartzenberg, that, unfortunately, he cannot make the journey to Europe again on Professor Schleyer's behalf as he did the previous year (1877). He pleads work commitments in the Egyptian Delta. He indicates, however, that he is prepared to answer the court in writing if there are specific questions they wish to put to him. —CG]

...Egyptian Christianity, as you gentlemen are undoubtedly aware, is, along with Syriac and Mesopotamian Christianity, the repositor of key elements of the heritage of early Jewish Christianity.

That is, among other factors, because of its geographic proximity to Palestine and the large Jewish population that resided in Egypt at the time of Christianity's rise.

By contrast, the Arabic-speaking Church of Palestine is, in ancient times as well as today, largely a Byzantine creation — the original Jerusalem Church having fled to Pella in Syria[1] during the siege of Jerusalem in the first Roman-Jewish war in A.D. 66–70. By the second Roman-Jewish war, the so-called Bar Kochba revolt, the native Jewish presence in Jerusalem, of whatever political or religious persuasion, had been largely eliminated. According to the sources, no circumcised person could reside there after Hadrian's time.[2] Hence, the Church of Jerusalem, such as it might have been in the second century, was wholly Gentile. Consequently, we must look to Africa, Syria, and Mesopotamia, if we are to catch the merest glimmer of the Christianity of the apostles and the first followers of Christ.

I'm writing this by way of pointing out that the Mar Yusuf myth, if I might call it that — the notion that the monks were guardians of certain traditions that could be traced to the family of Christ through James, bishop of Jerusalem — is not as far-fetched as it might seem on first glance.

Many objections can be raised to that thesis, of course, not least of which is that by the fourth century — the time of the writing of these codices — contemporary motivations existed that might account for them. Coptic, or native, Egyptian Christians were then attempting to differentiate themselves from the Greek-speaking Christians of Alexandria. One could propose the view that the Mar Yusuf legend would constitute a highly convenient polemic with which to establish the antiquity of Coptic practices against the liturgical and theological "innovations" of Constantinople and Rome, which were, even then, the source of considerable tension in Egypt — tensions that were to burst forth in full bloom a century later.

It must be said, however, that the argument that these documents are a species of Egyptian nationalist polemic is weakened by the fact that we have no evidence whatsoever that they were ever used by Copts in the various historical controversies with the other Christian sees over the Council of Chalcedon (A.D. 451). In fact, Mar Yusuf and its treasures are not attested at all in the literature that has come down to us.

---

1. Today Transjordan. —CG
2. A.D. 135. —CG

In addition, it is clear that the monks of Mar Yusuf, far from employing the legend in the service of some manifest "political" or ideological purpose, appear to have sincerely believed in the Joseph myth and to have lived in the light of that belief: namely, that they were, in some unique sense, as caretakers of the Joseph Archive, "sons of Joseph," the adoptive father of Christ — further, that they represented a definite Josephite strain until now unknown in the rich context of the spirituality of the desert.

As for the question of the community's origins, all we can do at this stage is speculate. The large Jewish population of the Fayoum and the strong Jewish flavor of the community's documents makes it likely that the founders of Mar Yusuf may well have been Jewish converts to Christianity. I suspect — and I believe Professor Schleyer would concur in this — that the archive's "builder" spirituality — namely, its appreciation of the mystical properties of the earth and of the spiritual character of the builder's art — locates these in a Fayoumite rather than a Palestinian milieu. The workers' colonies of Middle Egypt would provide us with both the religion and the craft of the archive's hero, Joseph.

Of course, there may be something to the legend suggested by the documents themselves — that an embassy from the family of Jesus of Nazareth deposited these texts, or some portion of them at any rate, with a Jewish-Christian community in the Fayoum — Professor Schleyer, if I'm not mistaken, allows for a possible Alexandrian setting as well, based on the six epistles to Jason — possibly in connection with the First Roman-Jewish war of A.D. 66–72. It is always possible, of course, though hardly likely, that the community included members — remote or otherwise — of the blood relations of Jesus.

For myself, I think had the Joseph Archive emerged in cosmopolitan Alexandria it would be difficult to explain why they had failed to attract the notice of the early Church. A Fayoum setting would make it possible for these texts, and for the community that revered them, to remain relatively obscure.

If this is so, what I propose may have happened is that a remote Jewish-Christian enclave in the Fayoum, probably declining in numbers by, say, the third century, may have been bolstered by an influx of freelance ascetics to the region during the height of the monastic movement in the fourth century. This new ingrafting on an already ancient tree promptly adopted the older community's

Josephite legends, texts, and at least some of its Jewish-Christian liturgical practices as its own. By the time of the Arab conquest in the seventh century, the transference was complete — the community of the Holy Joseph had become the Coptic monastery of Mar Yusuf....

2. Excerpts from the court transcript, May 7, 1878

DEFENSE: Fine. Professor, you were about to give us a brief summary of the history of the Mar Yusuf community when we broke for the midday meal. Please continue.

SCHLEYER: Yes. Well, when we left off, I believe I was telling the court that, to my knowledge, there's virtually no source material on the monastery outside the notes Eastman and I took from the nurse-monks of St. Menas before undertaking the expedition to the Fayoum.

PROSECUTOR: Convenient, that.

DEFENSE: Go on.

SCHLEYER: Thank you. That, of course, comes as something of a surprise.

(reading from his notes) "...We know that there were hundreds of monastic communities in Egypt during the great age of the desert fathers in the third and fourth centuries, when the youth of the empire went out to the wilds of Palestine and Egypt to continue in another form the spiritual hand-to-hand combat of the martyrs — against the anti-Christs, against the dark powers arrayed against the Gospel in the world. Not only did monks address the needs and ideals of the age, but the monastic movement was in every sense a mass phenomenon. In fact, Palladius, one of the early historians of the ascetic movement, records that by the close of the fourth century there were more than five thousand monks in Nitria[3] alone.

"These early monastic settlements exercised a remarkable fascination for the travelers and pilgrims of antiquity. For men and women dedicated to silence and retirement from the world, the monks and nuns of the Judean desert, Nitria, Scetis, the Fayoum, and many other locales were a well-chronicled lot. From the *Vita*

---

3. Wadi Natrun. —CG

Antonii of St. Athanasius to the *Verba Seniorum* to the *Historia Monachorum* to Palladius's *Lausiac History,* there's abundant contemporary testimony to the life of the desert solitaries and the communities that sprang from them."

So, why is it that we have yet to find ancient texts other than the Joseph codices that attest...?

PROSECUTOR: Please instruct your client that the phrase is "alleged codices"....

SCHLEYER: Sir, I am giving testimony. It is my belief that the four documents at hand are early codices. The court may choose to believe what it will. But I trust that, as a scholar, I may indulge my views.

DEFENSE: Friedrich, sit down. Calm yourself. We have been over this before.

PROSECUTOR: By all means, tell your client to indulge himself.

DEFENSE: Gentlemen, please. Continue, professor.

SCHLEYER: I was about to suggest three possible reasons why we find no independent confirmation of the foundation of Mar Yusuf on the basis of the ancient literature.

(reading once again from his notes) "...While the Fayoum is the setting for the call of the pioneer ascetic we refer to as Antony the Great[4] — a figure who held decidedly orthodox views — the region early on also gave rise to communities of Meletian schismatics, allies of the arch-heretic Arius, and numerous gnostic sects as well. Certainly, the ancient literature does not allow us to mistake the Fayoum as a popular place of religious pilgrimage on a par with Scetis or the Judean desert. Perhaps a vague sense of unease attached itself to the place. Despite the presence of important monastic centers, it seems to have been less explored by travelers.

"In a similar vein, the strong Jewish sympathies in the Joseph documents may indicate that the community of Mar Yusuf held views, or had a pedigree, that was considered suspect by some contemporary witnesses and was therefore bypassed in the sources.

"But, most importantly, a careful reading of the documents themselves, especially the marginal notes clearly attributable to the community, shows that the Mar Yusuf community held views

---

4. Antony the Great, or the Abbot, born in Upper Egypt, early pioneer of the monastic movement (A.D. 251–356). —CG

at wide variance with the standard doctrines associated with the leading ascetical teachers — though these views do not seem to be, in themselves, heretical."

DEFENSE: Such as, professor?

SCHLEYER: Their approach to demons, for one thing. If we put together the "atmosphere" of the documents with the things we know about the monastery's reputation locally, we get the impression that the monks of Mar Yusuf held views that saw elements of "holiness" hidden everywhere — even in evil, even in fallen angels. That would certainly distinguish them from the vast majority of monks who saw themselves as spiritual gladiators waging a never-ending war against the devil and his hosts in the world.

Such factors may account for the fact that Mar Yusuf is not attested to in the ancient histories of the desert. In any case, we are only just beginning to do really scientific work on the Egyptian monasteries — especially in Middle and Upper Egypt. In fifty years, scholars will doubtless be in a position to shed much more light on these matters.

PROSECUTOR: Your client surely isn't suggesting that it will take that long to ferret out the truth about this business, the Mar Yusuf affair, is he?

DEFENSE: I don't think he's taking a position on that. He's only telling us what he knows. Isn't that right, professor?

SCHLEYER: That's correct. Had we — Max Eastman and I — been permitted by the circumstances to interview Abbot Pambon before the early morning raid on the monastery,[5] we would certainly know a great deal more than we do. The documents at hand give only indirect testimony to such questions as the origins of the community and what its pattern of life may have been like. Still ...

PROSECUTOR: But, if it please the court, there's a basic issue here that's being evaded by this testimony — *fascinating* as it all is. And if we're to get through the professor's declarations by nightfall ...

DEFENSE: Evaded?

PROSECUTOR: Evaded. As in what pugilists do when they bob and weave. Mr. President, may I be permitted to address the accused? Thank you. Professor, whatever the relative merits of your declarations about what you allege you heard once upon a time from alleged monks in Alexandria about an alleged monastery in

---

5. August 17, 1874. —CG

Middle Egypt, were you not, in fact, asked to do a great deal more for the court in this session than read your notes on Mar Yusuf into the record?

SCHLEYER: I...

PROSECUTOR: You were requested, sir — I am quoting the court order — to "provide the court with hard evidence of the monastery in question's existence and any other historical or other background information that may be helpful in establishing the authenticity of your claim in the form of locally certified affidavits posted from Egypt" — not to you or Mr. Eastman — but "directly to the president of this court."

DEFENSE: But you have numerous notarized declarations on Professor Schleyer's behalf right in front of you.

PROSECUTOR: Yes, as a matter of fact I do. And I must say they're a pretty disappointing lot.

SCHLEYER: Sir, may I....

DEFENSE: Friedrich, let me handle this.

PROSECUTOR: A disappointing lot from the court's point of view. They all stress Mr. Eastman's credibility with the local authorities as an antiquities field director. Fine. But virtually none of these references has a single word that addresses the question at hand: whether reliable officials — local and/or foreign — will attest in writing that Mar Yusuf is known to exist.

SCHLEYER: Sir, you know very well that the affidavits were never intended to be anything more than personal references. We had hoped to allay all suspicions about the "question at hand," as you put it, by summoning here to Breslau...

DEFENSE: Friedrich, please. We had agreed. I can't help you if you...

SCHLEYER: ...by summoning here to Breslau a surviving member of the community who was located a few months ago in Alexandria.

PROSECUTOR: Yes, there had been rumors of something like this... but now that we have it from your own lips...

DEFENSE: Gentlemen, I wish to call a brief recess to confer with my client.

PROSECUTOR: As you wish, counsel, but the damage, as they say, has been done. Professor, this is most interesting. One might almost call it a "sensation." We assume, of course, you have booked this sterling and irrefutable piece of evidence passage on

one of our efficient German steamships, perhaps even the luxuri-
ous *Berenice,* given the importance of this affair for the question
of your own freedom of movement, let alone reputation. But perhaps the good father is already resting at your hotel, waiting only
for the summons to appear before us. Who knows, he may, even
now, stand at the hearing room door — a man of Mar Yusuf, a
man of the fourth century ready to confide all his secrets. I really
must apologize, professor, for letting my suspicions run away with
me. Who would have thought you would prove capable of turning
water into wine at this late date?

Well, professor, we're all waiting. Where's the monk?

DEFENSE: I demand, I demand a recess...

SCHLEYER: There is no monk.

DEFENSE: Oh, God.

PROSECUTOR: Really? No monk at all? None? Whatever do you
mean, sir? Surely you're not telling us that the monk of Mar Yusuf
that we were promised was a mirage... like everything else?

SCHLEYER: I mean that the monk is dead....

3. From Affidavit #5, Sent by Maximillian Eastman to Dr. Klaus Schwartzenberg, President of the Court, Breslau, from Alexandria, May 1, 1878

... Sir, I can only say this, outside of our phenomenal good fortune in happening upon the Joseph documents themselves: the
Mar Yusuf venture has been a luckless business from the start. The
burden of its attendant misfortunes has fallen firmly, and unfairly,
upon the shoulders of the one man who wished only to share what
he had found with the world: Friedrich Schleyer.

One learns quickly in life that misery comes not through malice
but through mishaps, accidents for which one can neither prepare nor adequately defend oneself. It is this, more than religious
doubt, that causes one either to disbelieve in gods or to conclude
that they are not worthy of the effort.

On to the latest instance of divine mischief in the drama of
Mar Yusuf: the business of the death of Brother Mark, a surviving
member of the Mar Yusuf community, in Alexandria, on April 15,
1878.

Through Father Amnon of the nurse-monks of St. Menas, one of my most trusted advisers in Coptic affairs, I had sought and located one of a handful of survivors of the devastating raid on Mar Yusuf of August 17, 1874. Having escaped with his life, but little else, an elderly monk had managed to make his way to Taposiris near Alexandria and was given refuge at the monastery there.

Amnon informed me of his presence there and secured the monk's willingness to cooperate in the effort to establish the authenticity of both his community and its treasure. Brother Mark — that was the monk's name — proved to be in the best possible position to do so in that he had functioned at Mar Yusuf as its librarian and was well-acquainted with the Joseph codices and their contents. His loss is incalculable not only to our cause in the hearings now under way but to an accurate and fulsome understanding of the codices themselves.

I will not bother to tell the bitter tale myself, but have attached the letter from Father Amnon informing me of the tragicomic circumstances of the old man's demise.

Alexandria
April 17, 1878

My dear Mr. Eastman:

It is with great regret that I am compelled to inform you that our esteemed brother Mark, late of the monastery of Mar Yusuf, has fallen asleep in the Lord. It happened night before last, between the hours of the Midnight Office and the dawn.

Brother Mark, it seems, had been raised a farmer's son in the Fayoum and was loath to accept the comforts that we Alexandrian monks take for penances. Although an old man, he was in the habit of wearing a simple cotton robe, never so much as permitting a cloak or mantle to warm him, even in winter. He had never once known illness of any kind, he told us.

"A farmer's son must feel the air on his skin," said he.

When we determined that his talents would be useful in Alexandria, we moved him to Taposiris when he could help catalogue our library there. (As I believe I informed you, Brother Mark had been the librarian at Mar Yusuf for many years.)

Well, as you, my colleague, know, the air is damp in Taposiris. The abbot there, knowing the troubles a wet climate can bring on old bones, urged the monk to wear a warm woolen mantle. Brother Mark refused, saying that if he had not seen the need to fend off the mists of the Bahr Yusuf with extra clothing, he would not require it for sea breezes.

For months, the monk refused these urgings. Finally, exasperated and fearing the onset of the later rains, the abbot no longer urged, but ordered him to wear a large woolen cloak.

Faced with this, Brother Mark obeyed, whereupon he promptly caught a chill and died.

As the Psalms say, "On that day a man's plans perish."

Great regrets,
AMNON

4. Memorandum on the subject of the Mar Yusuf community by Constantine Gruber
"Notes toward a Translation of Echoes"

[*Note:* The "official" tone of these reflections suggests that Gruber intended to publish an essay on Mar Yusuf at some point, based on these jottings. Another aspect of the tone of this excursus — its "softer," less cheerfully abrasive, less skeptical atmosphere — would appear to date it toward the end of Gruber's dealings with the Joseph Archive, somewhere in early 1951, shortly before the scholar began his fateful correspondence with the monks of St. Menas. —Ed.]

Egyptian monasticism has a peculiarly personal relevance for this scholar in that it was by way of a visit to a Coptic monastery in the Wadi Natrun in the year before the war that I first decided to involve myself in Coptic studies.

Like most Egyptian specialists, I had been initially attracted by the study of Pharaonic Egypt — barely aware of the rich heritage of Christian Egypt that grows, even today, in its ruins. My specific interest was Egyptian magic and the study of amulets. Outside of the British Orientalist Sir Wallis Budge, no one had done much work in this area, and, of course, young scholars have their eyes peeled for scholarly avenues through which they might make a quick name for themselves.

In the spring of 1939, the German Archaeological Union, of which I was then a member, sent me on a fact-finding mission to the Wadi Natrun, a depression northwest of the resthouse between Alexandria and Cairo, whose foul-smelling natron lakes — hence the name — had furnished ancient Egypt with many of the salts and other chemicals used in the mummification process.

While there, I learned that the region had another claim to fame: namely, that it had played host to a chain of early monastic settlements, more than one hundred before the Arab conquest, several of which were still inhabited.

That was how I came to visit Deir Baramos (Monastery of the Romans), the northernmost monastery in Wadi Natrun. Less famous than its neighbors, the Monastery of St. Pschoi, seat of the Coptic patriarchate, and Deir el-Suriyani (Monastery of the Syrians), the high-walled enclosure is named for Saints Maximus and Domitius, brothers and Roman soldiers who had sought the counsels of the area's great spiritual light, Saint Macarius (A.D. 300?–390). After their deaths, but a few days apart, so tradition says, Macarius had a shrine erected here in their honor.

The monastery had about fifty monks at the time when I visited it. (God knows what the dislocations of the war have done to the place.)

Prepared to find a single monastic structure with a central church and cloisters as in Europe, I was astonished to encounter at Deir Baramos nothing less than a form of the monastic laura or village of the earliest centuries of monasticism, albeit walled for protection against marauders.

The monastic laura was, of course, the "mother" of all monastic architecture; but, in European Christianity, at least, the growing diversity of the forms of Catholic religious life early on necessitated other institutional settings.

Here at Deir Baramos, however, the outlines of the early Pachomian village were still discernible. Modeled on the Roman military camp, the monastic settlement was meant to be a self-sufficient community: There was a watch tower set in an enclosing wall, a gatehouse, a guesthouse, a main church, a refectory or dining hall, with a kitchen nearby, an infirmary, and, at least in some of the ancient Egyptian settlements, a number of separate barracks blocks in which to house monks, or, in the older monasteries, individual house-cells. Hermits normally lived in nearby caves or rock tombs and were supported by the community.

(While no one in his right mind would wish to describe life in these climes as less than rigorous, most of the ancient monasteries, Deir Baramos included, were set up around wells, on the edge of desert oases and often within sight of settled agricultural communities where food could be purchased and monastic wares sold.)

Deir Baramos was laid out along these same lines. The compound could boast not one but five churches, dedicated to the Holy Virgin, St. Theodore, St. George, St. John the Baptist, and, appropriately, St. Michael the Archangel, situated on the second floor of the monastic keep or three-storied watch tower. (The archangel is traditionally featured in iconography as the defender of Christians.)

There's a refectory where the monks share their one weekly communal meal, next to which is a baptistery and an olive press.

Deir Baramos also has the requisite three palm trees in its central court upon which whips are still hung for the punishment of monastic malefactors and less agile thieves.

But, I discovered, these ancient foundations possess other unique characteristics. Unlike the cloisters of the West, which have often appeared — and have been, in fact — physically separated from extended contact with common people, the Coptic monasticism I encountered was not only a living spiritual force but one deeply and organically connected with the concerns of lay people and, indeed, the most practical cares of the local peasants.

For one thing, the wisdom of Oriental monasticism was, and is, conveyed not through the apparatus of the Academy — the treatise, the manual, the polemic — but through the staples of popular culture: folk stories and sayings.

As in ancient times, city dwellers from Cairo and Alexandria could be seen mingling easily with peasants in their long blue galabiyehs as they lined up for a "word" with a monastic elder of repute before Vespers and on feast days.

(The farmers, one young monk who had studied in Germany confided, have more prosaic concerns: the best kind of fertilizer to use on a natron-soaked topsoil, or how to settle a dispute over irrigation rights.)

Local women feel free to invade the cloister on Saturdays with their armies of well-scrubbed children looking for a monk to instruct them and then, that attended to, spread out their colorful blankets in the monastic enclosure for a leisurely picnic laced with gossip and laughter.

No one — priest or peasant, it would appear — has denied himself that most Egyptian of virtues: a hearty and deeply ironic sense of humor.

And yet the monks are nothing if not serious about their ascetical regimes, treating themselves to long seasons of fasting during the year, coupled with retreats to nearby caves for even stricter seclusion, to pursue life for a season, or forever for that matter, as an anchorite, a hermit, one who has, as a young monk put it, "disappeared into the heart of the world."

Admittedly, these are the surface impressions of a mere two-day excursion. But they have proved durable. Here at Deir Baramos all was patient continuity — from the traditional forms of ecclesiastical art to a tenacious loyalty to an ascetical ideal of life — prayer, penance, and the pursuit of God — born in the troubled bosom of Late Antiquity.

Here in the presence of men who might as well be three thousand years old, I felt transformed. Why dedicate myself to the study of the relics of the past, I mused, when Coptic monasticism afforded the opportunity to examine a past that had managed to deliver itself whole into the present?

Weeks later, in Alexandria, I switched the focus of my studies to Coptology, with a specialty in the language within which the heritage of Pharaonic, Graeco-Roman, and Christian Egypt had been so richly mixed.

I mention all of this by way of personal background. But, of course, it goes without saying that the elements that characterized Deir Baramos also aid us in appreciating the nature of the life of the now-vanished community of Mar Yusuf, which, similarly, had its roots in the fourth-century spirituality of the desert (and perhaps something older still) and that had also survived into relatively modern times....

[*Note:* The essay appears not to have been completed. —Ed.]

5. Fragment of a note by Constantine Gruber

The following note was attached to the previous page by staple.

. . . Schleyer and Eastman state that there is no reference to Mar Yusuf in the ancient sources on the desert fathers. However, Helmut Berger (Toppler's generally wrongheaded, if enthusiastic, addition to our little research team) may have managed to make himself useful to the world of scholarship, after all. He's unearthed a possible exception to that thesis in the form of an incident mentioned by John Moschcus in the *Patrum Spirituale,* which concerns a demon residing in the cell of the great desert master Evagrius Ponticus (died A.D. 399).

So the story goes, a visiting monk from a "proud house" (that is, a "suspect" brotherhood) was invited by an abbot of Cellia (near Wadi Natrun) to stay in the holy cell of Evagrius. He did this not because he wished to honor the guest, but because he knew that the demon who had "misled" Evagrius was still there.

(It seems that several years before, a visiting abbot had insisted on the privilege of praying through the night in Evagrius's cell only to be found hanging from the ceiling when they came to summon him the next morning. For this reason, the abbot suspected that Evagrius's demon was still there.)

Thinking to humble this "son of pride" (a member of a "dissenting" community?), the abbot insisted that the guest be allowed to spend the night in Evagrius's cell — "for it was said of this [the guest's] brotherhood that they prayed for the souls of the demons. It was said that they prayed these prayers on the Monday after Pentecost."

But the visiting monk refused three times to consider it, saying that he was unworthy to so much as darken Evagrius's door. But the abbot compelled him. By next morning, the monks had already dug his grave when the guest appeared at the Morning Office alive and well. He thanked the community for their hospitality and the signal honor they had accorded him.

When asked what had transpired during the night, he said only that he had meditated with great profit on the phrase, "Remember not the sins of my youth." And all the monks were amazed. But some grumbled that devils enjoy the company of their own kind. These interpreted the phrase from the Psalms upon which the monk meditated to refer to the fall of Lucifer, the greatest of all the misdeeds of youth — that is, the youth of the creation.

While nothing in the story identifies Mar Yusuf by name, it is certainly possible that the "house of pride" referred to in the account is Mar Yusuf, since, as it turns out, the Josephites were popularly said to entertain hopes for the reconciliation of all to God in the end — even the deepest of God's enemies, the devil and his angels.

Since the early ascetics saw themselves as spiritual athletes contending with the forces of evil that gather in waste places, a community that took another, less aggressive, more integrative view of the nature of spiritual combat would inspire hostility.

One of the interesting points of the story has to do with Evagrius Ponticus, who did teach the doctrine of apocatastasis, or the universal reconciliation of all things in God — including the devil — at the end. (Hence, the "misleading" demon of the story.) The teaching appears to have been defended by Origen, the great third-century Alexandrian thinker, and was held in some form by early Church Fathers St. Gregory of Nazianzus, St. Gregory of Nyssa, Didymus the Blind, Theodore of Mopsuestia, and others.

There's no clear indication in the Mar Yusuf documents that the Josephites held a strict view of the matter of universal reconciliation. They appear to have entertained it more as a fervent hope than as a positive doctrine. Interestingly, in view of the allusion in the story to the prayers of Pentecost Monday, Orthodox scholar Paul Evdokimov contends that the Byzantine liturgy's "Kneeling Prayers" of the feast of Pentecost contain hints of a plea for the redemption of the damned. For example, the Third Kneeling Prayer contains these words:

> "O Master almighty, God of our fathers, Lord of all mercy and creator of all things living and non-living and of all the nations of the world: You have power over all. You are the Lord of life and death.... On this perfect and salutary feast, make us worthy to utter supplications in favor of those imprisoned in Hades, O Lord...."

However that may be, mythically it makes perfect sense: on the day when Christ has sent down the Holy Spirit on the Church below, the Church, duly empowered, sends down grace on those below — namely, on the world of Hades. On the day of the

Church's triumph when the Spirit of God itself is imparted, the Church summons the courage to utter its boldest plea.

6. Excerpt from letter to Alois Schleyer from Friedrich Schleyer, dated June 18, 1878. Postmarked Brest.

[*Note:* Alois Schleyer, the reader will recall, was the nephew of the discoverer of the Joseph Archive, who, according to Schleyer's published diaries, accompanied the Schleyer party on the expedition to Mar Yusuf in 1874. It is not clear how Gruber came to have access to this letter. Perhaps security agents of the East German police commandeered it from the Schleyer family records. At any rate, it is the last known correspondence from Schleyer before his presumed death later that year. —Ed.]

...Am I bitter, you ask, about the Joseph texts we so triumphantly stored in our stateroom on the *Finland* one summer morning in the port of Alexandria? Bitterness is not the word for my present state of mind. In the great scheme of things, I am little Creusa, daughter of Creon of Corinth, who unwittingly has received a gift of gold from the gods only to find it enchanted with evil magic. I am not bitter, Alois. I am burning, destroyed.

Proud men should never touch pure things made by magicians. Remember that, nephew. The humble have terrible powers at their disposal.

Our expedition to Mar Yusuf four years ago has left me with but one small comfort here, as I hide from the lawyers and their agents, the police. (Even my simple meals cost me twice as I must pay for errand-boys to sneak bread and sausage up to my room.) It is a strange comfort, having little to do with the purpose of our journey: a comfort of music. I still recall with such pleasure the singing of the monks as they prayed at the foot of the altar that night. In my many hours of solitude here, I've even tried to write it down: the hymn they sang that night. But I find even that eludes me. It is only the quality, an echo of the atmosphere of that singing that remains.

I hear it best, most accurately, in the midst of sleep, I think: that deep manly drone, so quiet, so elemental that it might be wind and not a human sound at all, a sound most like the English word "awe" held forever in suspension, above which the cantor soared on thin wings that dipped and trembled in the air:

"O noble Joseph, ... "

It is a music that seems at once fresh as dawn and old as Adam's first attempt to mimic the sounds of nature. I've been unable to bear the noise of the brass bands I hear from the streets since then. All our European music seems to me not to partake of the spirit of that chant, but to forbid the hearing of it.

In the presence of that music, something seems to break open inside, and I awake in the morning washed in tears. You remember me speaking to you about it, don't you, Alois? You remember....

Chapter 4

The Pilgrimage of
Three Tales

Notes by Friedrich Schleyer

This account of an incident during the journey of the Holy Family to Jerusalem for Passover given in Luke 2:41–52 is said to have derived from the early Christian martyr Conon, put to death in Asia Minor during the reign of the emperor Decius (A.D. 249–51). His "acts" indicate that the martyr affirmed in court that he was "of Nazareth in Galilee, of the family of Christ, to whom I offer a cult [of worship] from the time of my ancestors."

The attribution to St. Conon assumes, of course, that the account set down in his name preserves extra-biblical Nazarene traditions about the first famous Passover pilgrimage of Jesus when he was a boy of twelve.

However that may be, a marginal notation at the end of the work indicates that the document was not put into its present form until sometime in the fourteenth century by an anonymous penitent who referred to himself as "The Gatekeeper of Christ." Little more is known of him except that he may have been a Christian forcibly converted to Islam who functioned as a porter at Mar Yusuf. Interestingly, there are hints from a fragment attached to *The Prayer of Joseph in the Mikveh*[1] that our gatekeeper-editor may have had a son, bedeviled by tragic musings, who committed suicide.[2] It may be that he sought comfort in the example of Joseph.

At any rate, the hand of an editor may account for the relative literary sophistication of the text as we have it. The editor was clearly a poet of some sort, a rarity — or so it would appear — in the milieu of Mar Yusuf. *The Pilgrimage of Three Tales* has about it almost the feel of a primitive novella — a little like the King David sections of the biblical Books of Kings or the Pauline episodes of the New Testament Book of Acts.

The tales themselves would appear, then, to be the oldest stratum of text, embedded, as we have it here, in the ample "novelistic" setting of the "Gatekeeper's" prose.[3] The work's ti-

---

1. Now missing. —CG
2. There is also a reference to it in a marginal note that concludes the book, a note that, for some reason, Schleyer failed to translate. —CG
3. "Josephite" glosses are, as before, set in brackets. —Ed.

tle, "The Pilgrimage of Three Tales," would appear to reflect Mar
Yusuf's principal use of this text — less as scriptural elaboration
or "historical supplement to the Gospels" than as mystical allegories. The monks' approach to these texts would, on the face of
it, not be dissimilar to the way the Bratslaver Hasidim have traditionally employed the famous thirteen tales of Rabbi Nachman
(1772–1810): namely, as sacred stories in the manner of Solomon
and other ancient practitioners who "hid lofty and mighty con-
cepts in tales" (Nathan of Nemirow, Introduction to *The Tales of
Rabbi Nachman,* 1814).

The journey as scene of revelation is, of course, a traditional
biblical device. Many of the theophanies of the biblical patri-
archs occur in the contexts of journeys (Gen. 12:1–9, the call
of Abraham, Gen. 28:10–22, Jacob at Bethel, for example). And
then, of course, there is the Exodus event — Israel's deliverance
from Egypt, gathering at Sinai to receive the Law and the forty
years of wandering in the desert — paradigm of such journeys of
disclosure.

INTRODUCTION

Joseph the Builder descended into silence three times during his
earthly sojourn; three times did he refrain altogether from speech
(that is, outside what was necessary to maintain the conduct of
life and to obey the precepts).

The First, and lesser, Silence was when he learned that his betrothed Miriam was with child. The Third, and greater, Silence
came upon him when he fell asleep, that is, when he died in the
year before his son Joshua was "revealed," that is, when he began
his public ministry.

This history relates how the second of the three Silences came
about.

❧

Joseph and his son Joshua stood on the shore of the Sea of Galilee,
at the place the fishermen call the Seven Springs. Wellwater rich
with plantlife gushed into the lake attracting schools of the Amun
ha-Galil, mother-fish of the Galilee. When the older man saw their
fins breaking the surface of the water, he could not restrain a
phrase from a folksong about them coming to his lips:

"O poor man of Galilee, poor man,
do not despair, do not despair,
in the mouth of the mother-fish of the Galilee,
you will find a gold piece there."

Jesus, who is Joshua, remembered this saying later when he commanded his disciple Simon (Peter) to "cast a hook and take the first fish that comes up and when you open its mouth, you will find a shekel for the poll tax."[4]

But few fishermen were about yet. Pale sunlight was just breaking over the high Golan plateau to the east. Only a few still mending their nets from night-fishing could be seen huddled around fires on the gray, pebble-strewn shore.

The surface of the sea beyond them was as smooth as a silver mirror in the dawn light. In the stillness the only sounds to be heard were made by the gulls, aroused by the smells of morning, and by the kingfishers that were making a great racket on the shore digging for insects in the reeds. The two of them — father and son — were silent, pensive as they took in the beauty of the lake.

The rest of their family's addition to the Jerusalem-bound Nazareth caravan waited at the town of Migdal five miles west where they had reconnoitered with other family members there and bedded down for the night. Joseph and Joshua had set out long before the dawn to Kfar Nahum on the northern shore of the lake to collect from the synagogue leader who owed them money.

The building contractor and his son had said little as they hiked over the well-paved Roman toll route between Migdal and Bethsaida. Joshua had contented himself with a single question: "Abba, father, why are we going to all this trouble to collect a bill? The caravan will get a very late start, won't it? At this rate, we won't even make the Jezreel today."

Joseph laughed. "We'll have plenty of time to catch up with the rest of the caravan, Joshua. The delay — it's for a good cause, after all. We are putting everyone out so that a poor man may not have to shame himself before the Temple moneychangers."

The builder went on to remind his son that he always took along enough money on the annual pilgrimage to Jerusalem to ensure that pilgrims of their party without the means to secure a

---

4. See Matt. 17:24–27. —FS

proper lamb for the Passover sacrifice would not be required to "make explanations" or, worse, sell something to an enterprising Nazarene to "cover themselves."

"You remember that I've sent four messages to Menachem of Kfar Nahum about paying for the addition to his house that Jacob and I built last winter. This money I'd earmarked for the pilgrimage, for tzedekah — charity."

"Why is it," the contractor smiled, "that a poor man will insist on paying immediately for the humble thatch roof you've replaced, but a rich merchant, if you permitted it, would delay until the resurrection of the dead making good on his debts?"

"But today we are the merchant's angels," said Joshua.

"Exactly, my son," Joseph responded. "Today we knock at his very door and by the time the sun is ripe on the hills, we will have made him just. We'll even increase the worth of his deeds. If God gives us the opportunity, shall we not attach his debt to the delight of the poor? Little does the man realize how truly rich we intend to make him today."

Now Joshua was laughing.

Joseph felt relieved. It hadn't escaped a father's notice that his son had seemed preoccupied in recent months, saying little, taking long walks in the hills by himself. Not that the boy was derelict in his duties or less skillful with a mason's hammer than before. But a look that had long left his face — that terrible loneliness that had filled his eyes as an infant, an unbridgeable loneliness, so pure, so absolute that one didn't even have language with which to describe or address it — that look had returned.

"Tell me again how the sea is fed," Joshua inquired.

The two had had few opportunities to travel this far east of Nazareth together, although, of course, Joseph himself had worked in many of the densely populated towns around the lake. Lore about the local Galilean or Samaritan or Judean topography, the flora and fauna, were the very stuff of their long walks together to and from the various building sites to which their work took them. The son knew such legends nearly as well as the father. But Joshua was always eager to hear what his father had to say.

Rooted in the features of the natural world, Joseph's discourses on the currents of winds, the flight patterns of birds, the contours of the terrain, the presence of underground water, the character of vegetation, were the result not only of his practical knowledge, but, still more, of his own simple, yet profound meditations on the meaning hidden in the world.

"The world around us is a great scroll unravelled from one end of the earth to the other," he would tell his son. "How one struggles to read the smallest portion of it!"

"Of all the seven seas," Joseph began slowly, his words burnished by repetition, "the Sea of Galilee is called the one the Most High made for himself alone. That is clear because it is shaped like a kinor.[5] And music, as is well known, is the All-Holy One's special delight." The builder outlined the shape of the lake with a sweep of his hand. "One can hear the divine favor in the music its waves make."

Joshua crouched on his haunches, inhaling the wind off the lake and listening to the sound of the freshwater lapping the shore.

"Besides," Joseph continued, "it's fed from up north, from the snows of proud Hermon, the highest mountain in the Holy Land, the mountain closest to God. Those bracing streams join the warmer waters of the sea at the estuary at Bethsaida — joining but never mixing, the cooler waters descending to the bottom of the lake like a hidden stream where, below the town of Rakkah, they rise to 'kiss the mouth of the Jordan,' as the locals say."

"The lake currents are dangerous, then?" said Joshua. "Close to shore, no," responded Joseph. "But in the heart of the lake, where the unmixing currents swirl, where warm earth waters meet the snow-cold purity of the skies, the lake is very dangerous. Fish in the Galilee are known never to spawn in the Hermon currents down deep. And every year a brave swimmer or two, lured by the beauty of the black-blue waters, is lost there."

Joshua suddenly grew deeply quiet.

"What's wrong, son?"

"Nothing, abba," Joshua replied evenly. "Your words caused me to remember something, that's all."

Joseph wanted to inquire further, but restrained himself. He had learned over the years not only to respect, but to positively guard his son's freedom.

"In the darkness when you asked if I could smell the lake when we came over the ridge," said Joshua, "before I could sense the

---

5. An ancient stringed instrument. —FS

smell of water in the distance, I could hear the voices of the drowned arising to me from the deeps."

Joseph, feeling a sudden chill, gathered his cloak about him. What must it be like, he thought, to hear such things — the hidden things of life and death that Miriam, his wife, and his son, Joshua, hear?

"Spare me this," he prayed to himself, recalling the sleepless nights he had spent holding his wife in the darkness as she shook with a pain that has no name.

Joshua looked back at his father. "Go on, abba. I'm sorry, I interrupted you."

"About the lake you mean?" Joseph said, placing his hand on the boy's shoulder. "You know the rest: how the sea pours its life out into the Jordan River, which, in turn, waters the whole length of the land, from Beth Shean in the north to the valleys of the Arabah."

"And this river that feeds us, where does it end up?"

"Its waters fall at last into the Great Salt Sea, where they turn brackish and die," said Joseph.

The silence resumed between them as they looked over the vista of water even then coursing through the earth from the place of life to the place that Arabs call the Dead Sea.

❧

THE TALE OF THE WEEPING ANGELS

And Joseph told this tale on the second night of the pilgrimage to Jerusalem.

The caravan had encamped near Nain in a grove of Tabor oaks known to locals as "The Four Sorrows," after a legend that King David had first heard here of the death of Jonathan, son of Saul, at the hand of the Philistines on nearby Mount Gilboa.

Joseph did not often speak publicly these days. But in his own house and among his kinsmen, he had a reputation as a master storyteller. On Sabbath eves, in fact, neighbors were sometimes known to crowd his door after the meal to hear him tell of the strange places his work had taken him, of the customs of the Gadarenes or the folkways of Samaritan villagers.

Not that the Builder was a popular figure in Nazareth. He was both feared and mistrusted: feared for his holiness and mistrusted on account of his wife. The circumstances of their son Joshua's birth had not been forgotten, making their every virtue, their every act of kindness, suspect. "An arrogant bunch" — that was what people said about them behind closed doors.

But because it was a warm night, nearly windless, and a place associated with Joseph's ancestor David, and because he was among kinsmen, people felt sure that Joseph would be moved to tell a story or two: perhaps even of King David or how the men of Naphtali found the sacred blue of the prayer shawl in the sea.

The men knew better than to pressure the Builder, though, as they sat around campfires. The strings of the storyteller would be plucked, if at all, of their own accord, "when angels stir them," as Jacob, the man's nephew, told the others.

What provoked Joseph to tell the three tales — tales remembered long afterward by Nazarenes, though forgotten even there today — was a question that arose in the company after they had sung, at the caravan master's urging, one of the songs of ascent, the Psalms sung by pilgrims on their way to Jerusalem.

"If the Lord had not been on our side —
let Israel say —
If the Lord had not been on our side
when men rose against us,
when their anger flared out against us,
then would they have swallowed us alive;
the flood engulfed us,
the torrent would have swept over us,
over us would have swept the raging waters … "

This was the hymn they were singing when a question arose among the men sitting around Joseph's campfire. A Nazarene known to have had connections with Judah the Galilean, leader of the guerilla bands fighting the Romans, wondered aloud whether they would all live to see the Gentiles punished in the end of days.

[This man, one Nahum the weaver, lived to be the scourge of the brethren in Nazareth in the days of the apostles.]

"Punished?" said Joseph from the midst of the circle. He said the word without emotion, slowly, evenly as if luring a child out of danger. "Are you so eager for that, weaver?"

Gentle laughter scattered through the camp as Joseph's reply was conveyed to those out of hearing, particularly the women who were congregating at the tent flaps.

"With all my heart," the man responded. "I shall curse my fate if I do not see Rome's sins burn her down. Surely, builder, the Torah urges us to hope for as much. Why else, on Passover, do we celebrate the ten plagues God visited on our Egyptian oppressors? Why does the Torah say that the prophetess Miriam danced with joy at the sight of Pharaoh's army drowning in the sea?"

There was general approval around the campfire for what the weaver had said.

Joseph took a stick and stirred the embers of the fire without saying anything. The men looked at each other and smiled, waiting for the Builder's clever rejoinder. The fire crackled in the night air.

"But have you not heard the saying, 'While Israel rejoiced, God wept'?" Joseph said after a long pause.

"It is true that the foolhardy Egyptians, driven mad by the enmity of Pharaoh toward us, pursued our forefathers even there in the midst of the sea. As it is written, 'Pharaoh and his host were cast into the sea.'

"But when the angels of Israel wished to join their celestial voices to the dance of the prophetess Miriam, the angels of the Egyptians rebuked them. They said to them: 'The people of Israel sing of deliverance, but can the universe rejoice at the sight of destruction? Are not these, too, these Egyptians, though wicked, the sons of grieving mothers, the fathers of innocents?'

"So all the angels — the angels of Israel and the angels of the nations — besought the presence of the Holy One, to see his face, to know whether he rejoiced at the destruction of the Egyptians or not. And heaven's veil was opened and they saw the face of holiness and it wept, crying out, 'My image lies drowned in the sea, and you, my sons, would sing!'

"And the angels rent their garments and sat on the surface of the sea like the white flowers cast into the Nile when a child is drowned, as it is written: 'I desire not the death of the wicked, says the Lord, but that he may turn to me and live.'

"The end of the ages will be like that, my friends: the unveiling, not of God's anger, but of his tears."

THE TALE OF THE PRINCE
AND THE PROSTITUTE

But Nahum pressed him further. "But what are you telling us, son of David: that God has the same regard for the unclean as for the clean, for the nations that rejected the Torah as for the one that embraced it? I fear to think what the elders of Kefar Cana would say to that!"

Joseph smiled and answered him this way.

"There was once a prince, the heir to the kingdom, who saw a prostitute walk by each day as he paced to and fro on the palace balcony high above the street. He was a splendid youth, pure of mind and body, and all held him in the highest esteem. But no sooner had the lad laid eyes on the prostitute than he loved her at once as he loved his own life. (The woman, though corrupt, was of surpassing beauty.)

"Now you will say, 'He loved her because he did not know what she was.'

"But how could he not know: Do well-bred women go about the streets with uncovered hair? Besides, he had summoned his chief bodyguard the moment he set eyes on her and had him inquire about her in the city. She had lived an evil life from childhood and was so notorious, in fact, that decent people were known to avert their eyes when she passed.

"But for the prince, all this was of no account. Despite her manner of her life, he saw the purity of her soul, and the knowledge of it ravished him utterly. Wounded by the mere suggestion of her shadow on the paving stones, his pain permitted him to catch a glimpse of the holy flame that burned within the darkness of her many vices. And he was entranced beyond reason.

"He sent his most trusted servant one moonless night to ascertain where she lived. As expected, the prostitute lived in streets visited by no decent citizen of the town, in the darkest streets, in a house provided for her by one of her panderers — one who ill-treated and abused her shamefully.

"On being informed of the particulars, the prince decided to send his beloved a token of his regard to see if her heart could still be moved by love.

"So, on three successive nights, he sent her gifts to prove his ardor and to reveal to her the identity of the one who loved her.

"On the first night, he sent her a cage of pure white doves. Laughing disdainfully, the prostitute opened the cage to the sky and let the birds fly away. (She was nothing if not a clever woman, knowing that refusing the first gifts of potential suitors invariably increases the value of those that follow.)

"On the second, he had an alabaster jar of expensive nard delivered to her — worth a year's wages. The jar she smashed at once on the ground, sending its perfume into the night air.

"And on the third, the final night, the prince had his servant present to her the royal signet ring, the ring of the kingdom itself. It was then that the prostitute knew who her suitor was and came to her senses.

"Was it calculation or repentance, you ask, that caused her to awaken? If truth be told, it was both. But in the light of the prince's trust, the light of her virtue was revealed and she saw at last the flame of her own purity. (This, brothers, is the genius of love: the revelation it affords of the beloved's infinite worth. It is this that drives the lover mad, like the prophet, and causes him to act boldly.)

"But fearing the wickedness of her owner, the prostitute sent a message written in her own hand to the palace:

" 'When you come to deliver me, beloved,' she wrote,
'do not come as a ruler,
arrayed in gold,'
(you see that she, though once dissolute, was deeply wise)
'but as a beggar, come,
as a beggar disguised.'

"The prince heeded her advice and came for her dressed as a drunken beggar, singing love songs in the street.

"Delighted, she went away with him, right under the slave-master's nose, and the prince brought her home with him into the palace. He called all the courtiers together with the king and queen and all his royal siblings, saying: 'Rejoice with me, beloved of God! Do you not see? My bride has come to me at last after a long, long journey! We must make a feast in her honor!'

"But all the palace murmured on seeing the noble prince dressed as a beggar with a prostitute at his side and their shock and astonishment knew no bounds. 'He has gone mad,' they said, 'we must restrain him, lest he pour our inheritance out on this slave!'

"And they began to conspire against him, how to bring him down and put another in his place, one who would protect their interests...."

At these words, there was a stir in the crowd, as a young figure, tall and well-built for his age, moved through the seated men to his place at the storyteller's feet.

"Ah ha," the caravan men cried, "*this* is the heir!" At that, the whole caravan laughed as the Builder's son, Joshua, kissed his father's hand and sat down beside him.

"Apologies, abba," he murmured as the Builder welcomed him. His mother, Miriam, also appeared now at the door of their tent and saluted his appearance.

"Hail, son of the covenant," she cried, her eyes shining.

She said this because, according to the tradition of David's sons, Joshua, now on the brink of manhood, was soon to celebrate his bar mitzvah in Jerusalem during the Passover festivities and present himself formally to the council of the family's priests there.

And now, having completed his duties guarding the perimeters of the encampment with the other men, Joshua took his place among the males of Nazareth for the first time.

A few of the women around Miriam, those of her family especially, began to whisper words of congratulation: "Blessings, Mother of Joshua, righteousness be his and many children in the day of the messiah!"

But others took advantage of the interruption to voice their displeasure at both Miriam and the gist of Joseph's story. "Can the Builder imagine we are not aware...?" they murmured. "He speaks of princes and prostitutes in order to justify himself."

Joseph, doodling with his stick in the warm ashes that spilled from the fire, waited some moments for the company to settle down once more and continued his tale.

"In the end," he resumed, "the prince's household succeeded in their aims. They conspired with the prostitute's panderer to discredit the prince in the city, and, though he was blameless, to accuse him of being a fornicator and a glutton.

" 'This man loves what is unclean,' they cried, 'and so he too must be unclean.'

"As for the prince himself, he did not prevent the conspiracy from unfolding, having only a single care in his soul: neither power, not position, nor wealth, but only the boundless love he bore for his chosen bride. In the end they cast him out of the house of his fathers to live with sinners and awarded his throne to another.

"And so, though a prince, indeed a king, he dwelt with his bride among the wicked, teaching her to redeem the hidden fires and raising up sons for a kingdom yet to be revealed."

ه

"I don't know, Builder," Nahum the weaver said finally, breaking the long silence that had blanketed the scene since Joseph's voice had trailed off. "It's a pretty enough story, but I, for one, am not convinced. Your 'prince,' if I may say so, has more the air of Zeus Atabyrios, whom the ancients used to worship on Mount Tabor, with his blind infatuations and his women, than the God of Abraham, Isaac, and Jacob."

The weaver spoke slowly, measuring his words. Never one to shy away from debate, he had no wish to anger the master craftsman in this setting, with his son present.

"It's the pagans surely who wish their gods to be...passionate."

Some of the men were inclined to agree with him and a few quiet murmurs of assent rippled through the circle of travelers.

Joseph, silent, his head bowed, continued to doodle with his stick in the ashes. Joshua, his head resting against his father's knee, noticed suddenly that Joseph had scrawled something there in the soot. He leaned over to see what it was that he had written.

A voice rose from the circle around the fire, singing in the fine even tone reserved for cantillations in the synagogue: *"Yeeshakaynee,"* the voice dipped and bobbed like a swallow, *"meensheekoht peehoo..."*

It was the voice of Joshua reading the words in the sand, a phrase from the Song of Songs, the poem of the nuptial love of God for Israel.

> "Let him kiss me,
> let him kiss me
> with the kisses of his mouth..."

There was silence for a moment and then everyone, Joseph, Joshua, the men, the women, even Nahum the weaver, laughed and laughed. They laughed until they hurt.

As things nearly always turned out in such cases, Joseph had had the final word.

THE TALE OF THE BOY
HIDDEN AMONG THIEVES

But it was on the third and final night of the pilgrimage, when the caravan had reached the tomb of the prophet Samuel, from which the first views of the Holy City could be had, that Joseph told his last and greatest tale — a tale greater than any that he had ever told before, or that he would ever tell again.

[This story that the Builder told that night was talked about for many years among the Nazarenes, and was the subject of much discussion among Joseph's relatives in Bethlehem. There are, even today, many versions of it among the family of Christ. This version of the event is the one that Conon the martyr knew, the one he passed down to the Lord's brothers in Aleppo.]

Scouts had gone out ahead of the Nazareth caravan shortly before *Ma'ariv,* Evening Prayer, to climb up the hill of the prophet Samuel and ascertain if the lights of Jerusalem could be seen in the distance west of the Moabite plateau.

Having spotted the Holy City, the scouts lit a bonfire of sirah, or thorn bushes, on top of the hill to alert the caravan below that Jerusalem, "citadel of the Great King," with its white alabaster mountain of a temple, lay in view, a mere morning's walk away.

"I rejoiced when they said to me,
'Let us go to God's house,' "

a knot of pilgrims sang when fires were first seen blazing on the hill.

" ... And now our feet are standing
within your gates, O Jerusalem ... "[6]

And as the company sat down for the last time around the campfire, Judas, Simon of Clopas's eldest, who was on his first

---

6. Ps. 122:1–2. —FS

pilgrimage to Jerusalem, asked the Builder to tell the story of the Nicanor Gate, the easternmost passage into the temple compound. Judas was referring to the fact that the craftsman had supervised the gilding of that gate six years before. [His old friend Jason of Alexandria had insisted that the Nazarene be involved in the project; the Alexandrian community had donated the gold.]

"They say, Joseph, that it's the most beautiful building on earth," Judas exclaimed, "a snow-covered mountain that has caught on fire!"

"Oh, yes, it's all of that," Joseph said at last. "All precious metals and alabaster and multicolored marbles! But do you ever wonder, Judas, why it is that the Most High, whose house it is, sits alone in darkness, in the depths of the Holy of Holies where there is no light at all?"

There was an almost audible sigh that settled over the crowd dispersed around the campfires. Before the streets of the Holy City claimed them for the feast, the Builder would seed their dreams just one more time.

"Once there was a king who had an only son," the storyteller began. "The child was so beautiful, so full of joy that sometimes the king wept at the mere thought of him.

"But the king harbored a greater love in his heart, greater even than the love he bore his infant son. More than life itself, he loved his kingdom, the people over which he ruled.

"His had long been a troubled land, but lately the scourge of bandits had been added to its catalogue of ills. Vandals from another province had swept down upon the people, plundering the towns and villages, ravaging the countryside without mercy. And all the king's efforts to apprehend them proved fruitless.

"One noon, overcome with anxiety from many sleepless nights, the king fell asleep on the roof of the palace. An angel appeared to him in a dream and revealed a novel and terrible solution to his dilemma.

" 'Place your son, your only son, in the midst of the thieves,' the voice said. 'Do this and all will be well.'

"When the king awoke, he promptly concluded that a demon had invaded his sleep and drove the idea from his mind.

"But the bandits became still more bold and made many widows and orphans, and the capital city soon filled with refugees clamoring for action from the king.

"At long last and with a heavy heart, the king reconsidered. As the angel had commanded, he consented to have his heir, his beautiful child whose eyes were alive with innocence, set among the worst of men. Perhaps, he said to himself, it is the will of the gods that the boy's goodness turn these wild beasts from their course.

[According to the testimony of Judas, given at Pella in Roman Syria, the "son" of the tale is Israel, placed by God in the midst of the nations. But James has it that the Builder meant the messiah.]

"So, one day the king placed the child alongside the main road, keeping a close eye on him from a distance. In due course, the bandits arrived at the spot. They were astonished to find a toddler there playing on a satin cloth, bundled in fine clothes with gemstones sown in the seams. Naturally, the vicious but quick-witted men knew right away that he was a nobleman's son. Perhaps he had become separated from his parents during one of their raids, they thought.

"A young thief offered to dispatch the child immediately with the butt of his sword. But the bandit leader said, 'You don't understand the situation at all! He will fetch a fine ransom once we determine whose family he belongs to. In the meantime, we will adopt him as part of the band. Perhaps we will even teach him how to be a proper thief.'

"So the king's son grew up among the thieves. As the months and years passed, his agility and cunning inspired some of the band's most daring exploits. [The boy's astonishing innocence dazzled the thieves.] And they praised their good fortune in finding the boy and grew bolder and more inventive in their crimes.

"As for the king, he lived on bread and tears and gave strict orders that no lamp be lit in his house by day or by night until his son should return to him and the angel's promise be fulfilled.

"Finally, one night as the king lay sleeping, the angel appeared to him again in a dream and said, 'Arise, my son, from the bed of your grief. You have done well in trusting my word and hearkening to my command. Now, listen to my words once more: Proclaim a feast for all the land and summon the people to the palace to eat and drink and be merry. Say to the people, 'Your cruel sufferings are at an end.'

"This time the king did not hesitate and, summoning his ministers, he proclaimed a feast for the whole kingdom. And all the people made their way on foot to the capital city, rejoicing as they went. 'The king must have driven the vandals from the land,' they cried. 'Why else should he call for a celebration?' And all roads were filled with dancing and singing.

"As for the bandits, they, too, rejoiced when they heard the news of the festival.

" 'What luck!' they said to themselves. 'Before this, we've managed only to feast on the spoils of the outlying towns and villages. With the proclamation of this feast, the palace itself is thrown open to us.'

"And so, disguised as beggars, the bandits joined in the procession to the great city as well. [The king's son, of course, was with them.]

"Once inside the walls of the city, the thieves jostled their way to the palace court where, they learned, rich food and drink were being dispensed to the people beneath the very windows of the king. There in the palace courtyard the bandits ate their fill of the king's provisions. All they wanted — rich meats and wine — were given to them without stint. And, of course, the thieves considered their plan of attack.

" 'Tonight's the night,' said the bandit chief. 'When all the capital is woozy with drink.'

"The king, meanwhile, in his bedchamber above the feast, had his eyes fixed on the courtyard, examining the faces of the children in the crowd, searching, searching for his son.

"Finally, late in the afternoon, when fatigue had nearly compelled him to abandon his quest, the king spied a small boy out of the corner of his eye, huddled in among beggars. While his countenance had changed — the king could hardly recognize the child at all in the grubby beggar-boy — the king knew at once that it was his son. The eyes gave him away, the eyes in which a father had once seen mirrored the reflection of his own soul.

"The king fell on his face, mad with joy and gratitude. And he called his servants and began to prepare the royal chamber for a late night visitor. [He knew well what was about to transpire.]

"By nightfall, the thieves were already gathering in the shadows beneath the king's bedchamber, poised and ready. They had hatched their plot: The boy would be lifted up to the low window of the king's bedchamber. Stealing silently in the darkness across the room, he would throw open one of the palace's outer doors to admit the thieves. 'The rest,' they told their young assistant, 'will be easy. In no time, all the treasure of the kingdom will be ours!' "

"Accordingly, they tied a long rope about the boy's waist by which he might send them signals should anything go awry while he was in the palace.

[So, too, do the associates of the High Priest tie a rope about his waist on Yom Kippur eve, lest he perish while uttering the sacred Name in the Holy of Holies and there be none worthy to retrieve him from the place.]

"That night the king, as usual, went to his bed in darkness — as he had done from the very hour that the decision had been made to sacrifice his son for the sake of the kingdom. Not a single lamp illumined the chambers and corridors of the palace. All lay in darkness. Even the moon itself hid behind a veil of clouds.

"At last, ascertaining that all the city lay wrapped in sleep, the thieves struck. According to plan, they lifted the king's son up to the palace window. He slid effortlessly through the lattice work and, without making a single sound, dropped onto the floor of the king's bedchamber.

"The room was pitch black. The boy could not so much as see the hand in front of his face. Moving like a gazelle through the darkness, he stumbled over something. Still, he made no sound. The floor was soft beneath him, soft as a satin cloth, and there was the sound of breathing at his ear.

"The boy felt in the darkness, to get his bearings. As he did so, his hand fell upon a face. It was all he could do to keep from crying out in terror. But the bandits had trained him well. He did not cry out. And, to his surprise, the figure he had happened upon in the pitch black room was silent too.

"His fingers grazed the contours of a fine noble brow and then onto eyelids that moved like gates of gold in the darkness. The lofty cheekbones reminded him of something he could no longer name, but the high thin line of the nose he grazed made him think, strangely, of his own.

"But it was when his fingertips happened upon the figure's lips that a word came to the child's mind, a very old word, a word that he had not said for nearly as long as he could remember:

" 'Father!' he cried."

For a moment, not even the elements could muster a sound to

compete with the Builder's voice, its volume rising steadily with excitement.

"This," Joseph said with triumph in his voice, "is why the Holy One sits alone in the darkness in the Temple, without light or lampstand: He waits for the son to return. This also is the meaning of the Temple and our journey toward it. Do the Psalms not tell us as much?

" 'Of you my heart has spoken: ... ' "

Joseph sang the words in a melody of lilting sadness.

" 'Seek his face!' "[7]

The caravan was deeply stirred. Never had any of them heard preaching like this, not even from the occasional rabbi from Jerusalem or Caesarea who might deign to divert himself from the delights of Sepphoris for a day's duties in a suburban village.

"Bravo, son of David," a few cheered. Walking sticks were setting up a tattoo of tapping on the hard earth.[8] Even the Builder's detractors could not withhold their admiration.

Suddenly a male voice called out, "But what happened to the thieves?"

The owner of the penetrating, slightly husky voice was not immediately familiar. Necks craned to get a better view.

"To challenge the Builder after such a tale!" — people clicked their tongues disapprovingly. Under the circumstances, the question seemed positively boorish, ill-mannered, like bawling out a folksong in the synagogue.

"The thieves, father — what did the king do to the thieves?"

Laughter drifted across the surface of the crowd. "It's the Builder's own son!" Older voices murmured, "Oh, Joseph, beware!" to more guffaws. "A child sits on your shoulder!"

The laughter, sparse, sporadic, was not good-natured. Nazarene men were considered not to be worthy to venture an opinion on even relatively minor matters until they were thirty years of age, and there had never been a village elder for as long as anyone knew below the age of forty.

Allowances had been made for members of the House of

---

7. Ps. 27:8. —FS
8. A kind of collective applause. —FS

David — "for the sake of the messiah," the elders said. But the Builder, who, as a young man had been consulted on various important matters, had always expressed himself with an admirable reserve.

Somehow one knew instinctively that this odd public exchange between father and son would not end well.

Startled a little at first, the Builder recovered his composure and looked for Joshua's whereabouts in the crowd.

The boy was nearby, sitting raised on his haunches, in the company of Mary of Clopas's sons, gazing directly into his father's face.

The Builder examined the familiar features for clues to the meaning of the intervention. There could be no question of bad manners or of idle curiosity — both were unthinkable in his son's case. (If Joshua had wished to question him further about the tale, he could easily have done so — and he often did — in the privacy of their tent.)

Instinctively, Joseph shot a quick glance in the direction of his wife, standing at the door of their tent. But there was no comfort to be found there. Miriam looked positively alarmed.

It was quite clear now to the Builder what was happening. His son Joshua, standing at the door of manhood, wished to complete the tale himself.

A slowly broadening smile spread over the face of Joseph. "O teller of tales," he said, employing the old formula he had used as a boy when urging his father Jacob to speak, "our ears belong to you alone!"

Joshua rose in his place and, bowing deeply toward the seated figure of his father, opened his mouth.

[*The Gatekeeper wishes the reader to be aware that the exact wording of the Lord's tale is uncertain. At the end of this book, you will find it exactly as it was given to this unworthy redactor, filled with deliberate misspellings and the insertion of misleading vowels and letters intended to render difficult, if not impossible, a precise reconstruction. The reader can decide for himself the reason for such precautions — although, once the tale is read, the reasons are not hard to fathom. The gist of the tale is clear, however, if not the exact words the Lord used. The writer has based his rendering on long study of the garbled page in question and upon consultation with Abba Moses the Thief, the oldest monk of the community, who had committed the tale to memory.[9]*]

"And the king kissed his long-lost son," Joshua began, "and while yet in his embrace, the boy revealed every detail of the bandits' plan to seize the palace treasure.

" 'Then, we must not disappoint them. We must carry out the plan,' the king said.

"So, as prearranged, the boy threw open the outer door to admit the thieves. And rushing into the palace, they fell straight into the arms of the king and the palace guards.

" 'It's a trap!' the bandit chief and his cohorts cried as firm hands bound them with the rope they had provided for the child. 'The babe on the road, the feast, the unlighted palace — it was all a ruse to capture us,' they fumed.

" 'The babe on the road," the king said, 'was my son. He is before you. As you see, he has returned."

"But the bandit chief answered back, 'It was this clever prince of yours who masterminded the scheme to plunder your treasure.'

" 'Nonsense,' the king replied. 'How can he plunder a treasure that belongs to him?'

" 'Take them away,' the king said at last. 'I will sentence these criminals at dawn.' As they were led away, the thieves cursed the boy who had betrayed them into the hands of their enemies.

"At dawn, the whole city was awakened by the king's messengers and told to assemble in the palace courtyard. Imagine their delight when they saw the bandit chieftain and his gang standing there in chains. 'So,' they cried, 'the king has really captured these rogues at last!' And they began to jeer at the thieves and mock them, seeing that swordsmen were close at hand ready to execute the king's judgment. (Remember how the people had suffered as a result of these men's crimes; how many widows and orphans they had made; how often the voices of the blood they had shed had appealed to heaven against them.)

"At length, the king appeared arrayed in all his finery, with his son standing at his side. And the ministers read out the decree

---

9. The "garbled" text of Joshua's tale does not appear among the Mar Yusuf documents. —FS

against the thieves, listing every one of their crimes in the presence of all the people. And there was not a single voice in the kingdom that did not shout for vengeance.

"Except one voice, that is, one small child's voice.

"As the king prepared to issue his sentence, his irrevocable judgment against the bandit and his gang, the prince stepped forward and said,

" 'Father, will you grant me one favor?'

"And the king, wishing to honor the son who had returned to him, replied, 'Of course, my son. The whole kingdom is yours. Anything you ask will be done.'

" 'As your word is law, then,' the boy said, 'spare the lives of these men and pass the sentence on me instead.'

[The boy realized that someone had to pay for the evil that had been done.]

"And there was shouting and consternation in the whole assembly.

" 'But my son, my son,' the king cried, 'you are innocent of their crimes. I myself, with my own hands, placed you among these scoundrels at the angel's word in order to bring them to justice and relieve the sufferings of the people.'

" 'Yes, father, that is true,' the boy replied. 'But you have accomplished more than you know: If you have created me the son of a king, you have also made me the brother of thieves.'

"This, the boy said, because he loved the bandits and owed his life to them, seeing that they had spared him when they found him and, despite their wickedness, had fed and clothed him.

"So, kissing his father's hand, the boy took off his royal garments and took his place with the thieves.

"And the king heaped dust on his head and tore his robes, knowing that he could not now go back on his word, nor remove the sentence he had pronounced. The king consulted with his lawyers for three nights and three days seeking to set aside the ruling, but there was nothing that could be done. The sentence and the promise were irrevocable.

"It was then that the king realized the full meaning of the angel's words: 'Place your son, your only son, in the midst of thieves and all will be well.' The angel had not said, 'and all will be well with him,' that is, with the son, but only that all would be well with the kingdom.

"The king called a fast and ordered his subjects to mourn for forty days. Until the very end, the grieving king prayed for a miracle, for the angel to appear once more and call a halt to the proceedings. But heaven was silent.

"And so in the dead of night, as the prince had requested, the thieves were released. Terrified now, they attempted to escape to their own land, but the people caught up with them on the main road and blinded them all. As for the boy, he was slain in the palace courtyard beneath the windows of the king. [The sound of his death cry became part of the kingdom's music, threaded through the most beautiful of their melodies.]

"The people, aware that this was innocent blood, and therefore sacred, had bowls of it brought to the countryside where they poured it out on their crops. As a result, famine, drought, locusts, and disease never again stalked the land. And the kingdom was prosperous and content at last.

"Every year, on the anniversary of the prince's death, the palace ordered that banners painted the color of his blood be paraded in every city and village of the kingdom to remind the people of the price that had been paid for their happiness.

"As for the king himself, he never again had the lamps lit in the palace and spent the rest of his days in deepest mourning."

Joshua remained standing as his final words sank into the fabric of the highland air. Dampness had all but reduced the campfires to steaming ash, and people were getting up to leave. They pulled their cloaks about them, unaccustomed, as Galileans, to the wet Judean breezes that would only grow more uncomfortable with each passing hour.

Many eyes, though, were still on Joseph. Early in Joshua's performance, people had found themselves studying the Builder's face. How would he react to such a dark, even savage revision, the spoiling of his once-edifying tale?

"Our little rabbi's boldness has been paid in kind," Nahum the weaver couldn't resist whispering to the caravan-master.

"A boy's words leave a bitter taste in the mouth," an old woman said just loudly enough for Miriam to hear — her eyes, like all the others, fixed on her husband.

Joseph's face gave nothing away. More observant Nazarenes, however, noticed that for some time the Builder had found it necessary to lean for support on his walking stick. In the absence of any further drama — Joseph remained seated, staring at the ground — the crowds around the campfire began to disperse.

Finally, the Builder himself rose, a little unsteadily, like a man struggling to his feet after a bad fall. Turning slightly toward his son on the way back to his tent, he said, with the barest hint of distaste in his voice: "A strange story, Joshua."

ॐ

No one in Joseph's tent slept that night: Miriam, Joshua, Joseph, all lay awake on their mats, unspeaking, their eyes open. None of them knew what to do — not now, not in the light of the evening's events. They were like earthquake victims after the shaking stops, uncertain whether they should remain still or flee, unsure whether or not something may give way beneath them with the very next footstep.

At firstlight, Joseph rose and did the morning ablutions at the well around which the caravan had circled. Only a few pilgrims were stirring.

"Blessed are you, O Lord, who restores life to the dead," Joseph murmured as he washed his eyes with cool water.

But the Builder could feel little of the morning's promise of daily resurrection — not after what had happened. The story Joshua had told around the campfire confused him with as yet nameless presentiments of disaster brewing in the city beyond them. What was he to do, the man commissioned by the council to "protect, guard, and defend the messiah" — especially when the messiah himself at manhood's door seemed to invite his own demise? In the crisp morning air, Joseph feared everything: Jerusalem, the Temple, the destiny of the Jewish people, the will of the Davidic elders, God himself.

He especially dreaded the moment when he must face *them,* Miriam and Joshua. All he knew was that he had to get away. Away from the caravan, away from the others. He had to try to think clearly. By noon, the caravan would reach the outskirts of the Holy City and the danger — whatever it might be — would be upon them.

Returning to the tent, he reached inside for his heavy wool mantle and walking stick, only to catch a glimpse of his son's eyes fixed on him in the darkness.

Joshua did not speak. But in his face, still marked with last night's look of quiet purpose, Joseph read the words: "I'm also afraid. But from this you cannot shield me."

&

The dark blue-shaded hillsides beyond the camp greeted the Builder with a spice-box of smells: the cool late spring sun had already coaxed wild bay and sage from the rain-soaked soil and scarlet poppies carpeted the land. Sheep bells jangled in the distance as shepherds herded their flocks out on the vegetation-rich slopes before the morning sun rose in the sky. But, for once, the charms of nature were lost on him.

All his senses were sealed.

The ashes of the last night's bonfires announcing the first sight of the Holy City were still smouldering at the top of the Hill of the Prophet Samuel when Joseph made his way to the stone platform from which pilgrims could scan the great vista to the south.

Jerusalem slumbered in the distance, still blanketed in shadows.

Voices from the caravan route below, the one coming from Jaffa and the coast, drifted up to him on breezes.

"If I forget y-o-u, Jerusalem," a lone old man's voice was wailing, amid the barks of the caravan master to the horsemen,

> "let my right hand wither,
> if I d-o not set Jerusalem
> above my highest joy ... "[10]

Sunlight spread slowly over the dark ridge of the Mount of Olives, highlighting Herod's great temple complex on the Mountain of the Sacrifice. Like a white lion, the Hechal, the Holy Place, crouched in the distance, tensing its muscles, as if it had spied a rival predator's approach.

For the first time in his life, Joseph found himself looking upon the city of his fathers, the seat of David's kingdom, not with the awe and devotion of the past, but with fear. In the space of a single night, it had become his enemy and the enemy of all he loved.

"And God said to Abraham ... "

The words of the *Akedah*[11] flowed into the Builder's mind as he pored over the features of the distant city: " '... Take your son, your only son Isaac, whom you love, and go to the land of Moriah, and offer him there as a burnt sacrifice on the mountain that

---

10. Ps. 137:5–6. —FS
11. "The Binding." —FS

I will show you.' So Abraham rose early in the morning and went to the place in the distance, the mountain that God had showed him. On the third day, Abraham looked up and saw the place far away. Abraham took the wood of the burnt offering and laid it on his son Isaac. And Isaac said to his father, 'The fire and the wood are here, but where is the lamb for the burnt offering? Abraham said, God himself will provide the lamb....' "[12]

There, in the distance, beneath Herod's marble, in the heart of the Temple, in the heart of Jerusalem, was that very mountain where the Father had been commanded to sacrifice the Son of the Promise, had passed the last and greatest of the ten tests to which the patriarch's faith had been put.

Almost before he knew what he was doing, the Builder forced himself down in the dust there in sight of the city. Scooping up clumps of soil in his large long-boned hands, he let the white chalky dust of the Judean highlands filter over his head.

> "Magnified and sanctified
> be his great Name in the world ... "

Through racking sobs, he choked out the words of the *Kaddish*, the mourner's prayer, the prayer of praise and submission,

> "which he has created
> according to his will ... ,"

saying the words as a man does when he loses an only child, when an only son is taken from him.

From that day on, so the Nazarenes say, Joseph told no more tales.

[*by the hand of the Gatekeeper who finished setting down this text of the holy Joseph on Nebi Samwil (the Mountain of the Prophet Samuel), at the Monastery of the Imprint, where the impression of the knees and feet of the Builder are miraculously preserved in the chapel floor. May the reader remember the Gatekeeper's son, a suicide. He prayed for death and it came.*]

---

12. Gen. 22:2–8. —FS

FRAGMENT OF A PILGRIM'S INVENTORY OF SITES ASSOCIATED WITH JOSEPH AND JESUS, BUILDERS

Carbon copy of a letter attached to the first page of the translation by Constantine Gruber

To: Niebel
From: Gruber
Date: August 16, 1950

I understand, my little Martin, that our superiors, wise beyond measure, are not altogether pleased with the fact that I've spent so much of my time going over Schleyer's work, over "previously traveled ground."

Such impatience. Like fervent nineteenth-century Anglican converts to Catholicism, your boys in the atheism committee really do want divine revelations over coffee and the morning paper, don't they? By the way, Martin, do you think you could get me some real coffee? Shortages continue for us here below, where, in the matter of coffee and cigarettes, ersatz is the word. God only knows what improvisations the coffee house owners are serving to us on the off days. And I don't want to know — ever — what I've been puffing on since 1944.

Be that as it may, Toppler and the lads will be pleased to see these pages, I'm sure, eager as they are, in the immortal words of their latest memo, for "previously untranslated material, ... virgin texts."

This, dear friend, is as virginal as it gets. Schleyer, for all his interest in the "pilgrimage" document, never even bothered to list this appendix to the main work, a charming little catalogue of locales purportedly associated with the contracting work of Jesus and Joseph in Palestine. (But then, he *was* in a hurry.)

So, I've taken the liberty to translate it myself. And you claim that my attitude is perceived as "insufficiently cooperative.... "

A few details: It was apparently put together by a pilgrim abbot of Mar Yusuf, Father Samuel by name — a woodworker, interestingly enough — who walked the length and breadth of the Holy Land in, I would guess, the early sixth century, certainly before the Persian Conquest in A.D. 614. He apparently spoke with some alleged members of Jesus' family in Nazareth during his visit and gathered whatever other information he could and compiled this list of sites where remains of the work of Jesus and Joseph could still be viewed.

GRUBER

❧

The monk Samuel, abbot of the Monastery of Mar Yusuf, graced by God to trace the steps of the God-man with his own bare feet in the year the Nile destroyed Thebes by flood, has written this. Not gifted by God with wit (he is a carpenter by trade), this poor chronicler is not able to write the many words necessary to tell all the wonders he saw with his own eyes in the Land of Our Lord. But for the uses of our monks who, God willing, may be permitted to make the pilgrimage, he has set down in writing this list of places where the sacred traces of our father Joseph's work, and things touched by the hand of the God-man himself, may still be found. By the merits of these relics may the sufferings of the many victims of the Nile's ravages be assuaged.

The author's guide on this journey was Phinehas, of the family of Christ through Simon, who lives in the house next to the Messiah's Synagogue in Nazareth where the Lord learned his ABCs and where one may find the bench that only believers may lift.

This is the catalogue:

1. In the vicinity of Bethlehem, near the Pools of Solomon, is the Spring of Eitam. There was once a village there, but the site is today abandoned. From the Spring of Eitam water once flowed to the Temple in Jerusalem by aqueduct to the ritual bath by the Water Gate. There the High Priest immersed himself before entering the Holy of Holies on the Day of Atonement. Phinehas showed me the ruins of a room that once housed the spring and indicated that the holy Joseph had designed the fifteen stone steps that still allow the visitor to descend into the spring to fetch water or to bathe — fifteen because there were the same number of steps leading up to the Hechal from the Court of Priests in the temple. Because the site is close to the village of Artas, where Solomon wrote the Song of Songs, Joseph is supposed to have carved the words, "an enclosed garden, a fountain sealed" — words from that book — on the surface of the stairs, but they have been worn away.

2. In Hebron, the city where David reigned for seven years before he became King of Israel, Joseph was commissioned to build a domed structure over the grave of Abel in the field where Cain his brother slew him. The previous building had fallen in an earthquake. This is in the place the locals today call the Valley of Tears because Adam and Eve are said to have mourned over the death of their son there for a hundred years. Nothing marks the place today except a large terebinth tree planted, it is said, by the Builder when he reconstructed the tomb.

3. Also in Hebron, on its heights, is a holy place called the Place of the Certain Truth. From there, one can see the deep chasm in which the Dead Sea lay below. There is a domed structure there atop the mountain in which one can still see the impressions of the knees and feet of Abraham the patriarch who heard from that spot the shrieks of the people of Sodom and Gomorrah as they were being destroyed by earthquake and fire. At this sight, Abraham threw himself on the rock and cried out in a loud voice, in lamentation for the inhabitants of the sinful cities.

Joseph built there a low wall to surround the sacred imprints. Only the lowest course of those stones is still visible today. Phinehas told me that Joseph had carved there on the wall the words: "The upper became the lower." By this he apparently meant not only the effect of the quake, namely, the falling down of the cities, but the abasement of Abraham, who did not rejoice at the fall of Sodom, but mourned for them with such passion that the stones still bear witness to it. It is said that this spot, among others, was a favorite place for Joseph to take the Lord, then a youth, to spend nights in prayer.

(This unworthy monk, too, slumbered there the whole night with wonderful results.)

4. In Jericho, there is a small church called the Church of the Palms, the atrium of which enshrines a portico, a columned aisle, erected by the Builder, although the locals, in their ignorance, claim that it dates from the time of Joshua, the aide of Moses! The portico, in fact, gives the church its name since the columns are shaped like the trunks of palms. Phinehas says that the aisle was constructed originally for a villa, from the ruins of which the church was built, and, more, that it was one of Joseph's later efforts and would have necessarily involved the assistance of Christ.

One can readily believe it since the columns, made of "sweet stone," the red limestone of Judea, are arrestingly beautiful. One can still make out just below the fluted capitals — very Egyptian in style — four names in Hebrew, one on each of the four columns: Rahab, the prostitute who sheltered Joshua's spies, and the three prophets said to have descended from her, Hulda, Jeremiah, and Ezekiel.

5. The family of Jason of Alexandria, father of the philosopher Philo Judaeus, contributed the gold for the plating of the great Nicanor Gate of the Jerusalem Temple. Because of the friendship Joseph enjoyed with the sage, they entrusted the Builder with the task of negotiating the transfer of the precious metal to the Temple authorities. When the gold plate did not adhere perfectly to the wood, Joseph supervised repairs on the gates at a site on the Mount of Olives. (He could not actually do the work because he was not a Levite.) This occurred when Christ was in his teens and served as his father's principal assistant. All that is left today of the Nicanor Gate is a portion of the stone lintel. A copy of the gate's design, however, is in the possession of Phinehas's family in Nazareth.

6. In Samaria, Jesus is said to have planted the twelve imposing mulberry trees that shaded the tomb of the patriarch Joseph in Sichar, one of which remains to this day. He did this to fulfill a commission his father had undertaken shortly before his passing.

Joseph is also said to have participated in the designing of a false sarcophagus that lies just above the true one to mislead would-be grave robbers from defiling the bones of the holy patriarch. (Bedouin had been known to raid tombs from time to time, looking for gold.)

7. Flavia Neapolis[13] boasts an ingenious aqueduct said to have been the last assignment in Samaria that Joseph undertook. It seems some villagers of Mabarakhtha, Aramaic for "blessed city," begged Joseph to design a means by which the poor of the village could have access to water from the springs on the slopes of nearby Mount Gerizim. According to the story, it was Christ himself who conveyed their request to the Builder. The rich landowners had built walls around the water sources in order to tax their landless tenants for the use of the water.

---

13. Nablus. —CG

Joseph, his son, and their assistants therefore built a series of tunnels that conveyed water from the hillsides to a pool within the poor quarter of the town, thus freeing the villagers from the tyranny of the landlords. For this reason, Phinehas declared, Joseph was forbidden to work again in that area. The tunnels and the pool can still be seen.

8. In the village of Zababdeh in northern Samaria, an exquisite capital carved with acanthus leaves is shown in the Church of the Theotokos there. The village is said to be named for the family of the apostles James and John, the sons of Zebedee. This column, it is said, once graced a synagogue that existed on the same site and was designed by Joseph early in his career, a portion of the first assignment, in fact, he took on after the exile in Egypt. The incomparable stonework design, in which the leaves of the acanthus seem almost to move as in a gentle breeze, was inspired, villagers say, by the Builder's love for the holy Virgin. Local Christian women rub the capital with their hands in hopes that their devotion will charm good husbands their way. Their fervor has managed to wear smooth the surface of one of the capital's leaves.

9. In Galilee, there are many sites associated with the career of the Builder and his son. In Kfar Nahum, the old synagogue boasted an elders' bench carved by the Builder out of a solid piece of basalt stone. With the building of the new synagogue there, portions of the elders' bench may now be seen in the Basilica of the House of Peter nearby.

A mosaic floor graces an inn there that is said to have been designed by the Builder. The design in white, red, green, yellow, and black tiles represents a field of six-pointed stars, the sign of the house of David. But viewing can be problematic. The innkeeper is certain that pilgrims wishing to see the floor have designs on his property — to turn it into a church. He has some basis for his fears.

10. The House of Studies next to the synagogue in Migdal on the shores of the Sea of Galilee was designed by the Builder. All that remains are fragments of the stonework that once graced the building, set now all in a row on the main highway so that pilgrims may venerate them on their way to Tiberias. It is impossible to convey the richness of the designs: pomegranates, wind-blown palm trees, grape arbors, rosehips, wild boars, springing panthers, cranes, hoopoe birds, pelicans, peacocks — all the living things of

the Galilee parade past the eyes. A convent nearby houses one additional relic of the House of Studies: in the chapel of St. Mary Magdalene is a stone tablet with Hebrew letters, said to have been carved by Christ himself. It reads: "In you [God] the fatherless finds mercy."[14]

[*Note:* The rest of the text is missing. —CG]

---

14. Hos. 14:3. This relic, like many of the others, appears to have perished when the Persians decimated the land in A.D. 614. —CG

Chapter 5

The Tamara Letters

Editors' Note

When this odd little work was in the proofing stage, we received a packet of letters at the offices of the *University of Leipzig Review.* Not antique ones, mind you, say from the time of Fredrich Schleyer and his adventures. That would have been too good to be true: "The suicide note of the tragic amateur archaeologist discovered at last in the wainscotting of an old tenement in Brest as demolition experts were arranging for the structure's demise."

No, nothing that good. But something, nevertheless. Our committee of editors argued long and hard over the idea of including this packet of fading handwritten notes from the late 1940s in our little "Gospel of Joseph" project.

Their relevance to at least the Gruber phase of things needs no defense. In fact, outside the correspondence found among the translations themselves, the seven rose-paper letters are the only existing confirmation that the minor Coptologist Constantine von Gruber, now unavailable for comment, even worked on these documents.

Nevertheless, the author of the letters contained in the manila envelope found in our post box one morning in late summer has not been located. Nor, from the look of it, does she wish to be. (We could doubtless initiate inquiries with our now highly cooperative security services, but that would cost money, and in foreign currency to boot.)

And, in any case, we had to admit that we had clearly invited this sort of "surprise" with our announcement in the East German student paper *Morgen* that we were planning the publication of the Joseph Archive and were soliciting information about the circumstances of its acquisition by the university and subsequent translation:

"Notice. The staff of the *University of Leipzig Review* is seeking the public's assistance in locating persons, documents, letters, and other witnesses — dead or alive — to the project called the Joseph Archive, once under the auspices of the late and unlamented State Committee on Religion and Atheism, but abandoned in the early 1950s under mysterious circumstances. Any information or material relevant to this inquiry will be welcomed. Confidentiality assured. Contact Johannes Slanova, *University of Leipzig Review.*"

So, making no claim whatsoever about the significance of these letters, the editors have, not without reservations, decided to publish them with the other texts under the title "The Tamara Letters," after the woman "Tamara" (or "Marra" as she more frequently referred to herself), who apparently corresponded over the period of several months in the year 1949–50 with Constantine von Gruber, translator of the Joseph Archive.

—EDITORS, *University of Leipzig Review*

The Tamara Letters

The following letters were deposited in the post box of the *University of Leipzig Review* on February 11, 1989. The seven letters, written on old prewar rose-colored stationery with watermarks (Italian-style), arrived in a manila envelope with a Leipzig postmark. A note in an elderly female's hand in the upper right-hand corner of the manila envelope read: "Publish them if you like. They can't hurt anyone anymore."

Letter 1

[in a woman's hand, scribbled hastily]

November 25, 1949
Flat 2, Franz Josefstrasse

Mr. Gruber:

Do not be alarmed. Nothing is amiss. I know your name from the mail box.

I have taken the great liberty of slipping this note under your door to urge you to keep our little secret between us. I don't need to tell you that, under the present circumstances, we may not survive without your discretion.

It was indeed foolish of me to have hid it, the crucifix, so badly this afternoon when I was cleaning the hall. Outside of yourself, hardly anyone in the building pays any heed to us as we women go about our duties as custodians.

And then this afternoon when you bent down to pick up the mop that had carelessly fallen from my hand, my poor crucifix tumbled out of my pocket, clattering on the floor. I assure you, it is the first time a thing like this has happened since the war.

If it had been anyone else, doubtless we would have been turned
in to the police immediately. But, even though we've never spoken,
you've always been so kind to the four of us these past months
since you moved into the Franz Josefstrasse: offering Hilda cold
water when the poor woman has had to wash down the staircases,
leaving an occasional extra ration of sugar or blue matches in the
custodian's closet (we all felt sure it was your doing!).

You have clearly guessed our secret. I could see that in your face
when I looked up this afternoon, when I went to my knees for the
cross. I must admit that the women of flat two spent much of the
afternoon getting their things packed, waiting for the worst, for
that inevitable bell to ring. (How is that one can always distinguish *their* ring from the half dozen others that bring one to the
door each day?) But when evening came and the police didn't, we
assumed that you had no intention of giving us away.

But, please, be discreet, Mr. Gruber and, for God's sake, do not
forget yourself and call one of us "sister" or otherwise defer in any
way to us, even when you imagine that you're unobserved. Surely
you understand how things are. The merest suspicion, and we are
lost. We feel sure that you understand.

By the way, was that you this morning playing the piano — the
piano part of a Brahms violin sonata, if I'm not mistaken, the one
in G major? It's been so long since we have heard real music.

Deeply in your debt,
SISTER TAMARA

Destroy this.

[On the reverse side, in a man's hand, Gruber's:]

Don't worry. Yes, I've known for some time. Have no fear. Your
secret is safe. And, by the way, I, too have a name. You needn't
call me "sir" anymore. I'm called Constantine.

I can help.

Letter 2

December 6, 1949

Constantine,

Yes, I suppose you're right. A man who puts his life on the line, has, at least, the right to know what it's all about, doesn't he? Sorry for not answering your inquiries sooner. As you can imagine, my situation doesn't afford me much practice in writing letters to gentlemen. I didn't want you to be misled in any way, that's all. We have already moved rather quickly in this "business" for my taste. But, then, you're a sensible sort of person, aren't you? Not like the others.

You will, in the necessary absence of any outward signs, keep things in proper perspective, won't you?

Yes, Constantine, the four of us staying in flat number two are Roman Catholic sisters, as you have surmised and my carelessness confirmed. The name of the specific congregation is not important. Not now.

What can I tell you? We have been on the run since 1943. Our superior came from a Jewish family, you see. She had converted to the faith while in university. That, by the way, is where I first heard of her — at the university. Legends flowed behind her as effortlessly as gossip in the wake of smaller personalities.

Oh, yes, she was a very persuasive person. That I can tell you.

Not many, even in the convent, knew about her background, of course. Mother Maria — that was her name in Religion — had discrete connections everywhere and no one bothered us for a very long time. But, eventually, the authorities got wind of her and that was that: We all had to doff our habits, split up in small units, and fare the best we could until the war was over.

I stayed with Mother Maria. We stayed together. Sometimes with other sisters for a time, sometimes just the two of us. Dark days, dark nights, always moving, never enough to eat, worries about the neighbors, recitations of the rosary in silence, whispered Little Offices of Our Lady on Saturday mornings, Mass at the backs of churches elbowed in among the faithful, sign language, special signals, always sleeping in your clothes, fighting off the urge to give in —

But then you're a decent person, Mr. Gruber. You probably

experienced something of that sort, too. You would know all about life in the shadows by now. Wouldn't have been caught dead working for *them,* right? Do tell me sometime what you did during the war, Constantine.

We have new masters now, of course. From the look of it, *you* have made your peace with them. (Please understand, I don't begrudge you that.) One thing about the old masters, though. They hadn't gotten around to thinking about Christians on principle yet. (That doesn't mean they didn't kill a lot of us just the same.) That, however, is where our new bosses have been more thorough: They have thought about us. And they have decided that we don't exist.

(By the way, you couldn't get your hands on a bolt of cotton cloth, could you?)

MARRA

Letter 3

December 16, 1949

Constantine:

Yes, I got your note, slipped in between the large yellow sponges in the custodian's closet as we had arranged.

"WHAT HAPPENED TO HER?"

(You're good at this, you know. You act on the basis that the worst will happen. That's a decidedly useful trait. I must say my confidence in you is growing.) And yes, your explanations were quite satisfactory. How nice to have been out digging up other people's pasts while the rest of us were digging our graves.

I know, I know, you're saying as you read this that I sound like a bitter old woman.

"You have no right to speak that way, you're not even forty" — that was yesterday's pronouncement from the Coptology Department, was it not?

You're right, you know. But it keeps the ghosts away, bitterness.

What happened to her? I have not thought about it for a long time. At night sometimes, I still wake up and think I see her stand-

ing at the window, looking out into the street, just about to turn
to me and whisper, "Oh, my dear, have I awakened you?"

What happened to Mother Maria: One morning she went out
to fetch a tin of tea — it was to be a gift for my feastday. If I'd
known what she had in mind, I'd have never let her do it. It was
far too dangerous for her to be out in the open like that. Her name
was on numerous lists. But an older sister who always went out
to do our shopping was ill that morning. I think she did it without thinking, or because she'd had enough of being "safe." I don't
know.

As for me, I was in the adjoining room, studying. Mother was
determined that I should somehow manage to keep up with my
language studies — even under the most difficult conditions.

She went out to get the tea and she never came back. We learned
later that a Gestapo dragnet had picked her up not two blocks
from our apartment. We still have no precise idea what happened
to her, although the Vatican is still making efforts on our behalf. Ravensbruck, Matthausen, Bergen-Belsen, Auschwitz. Who
knows?

Now some Polish peasant plows fields seeded with first-class
relics.

Shall I tell you something interesting about her? I once spoke to
her mother — that was in Bremen before the war — who claimed
that through the Turkish side of the family, Mother Maria was
a distant relative of Christ. Isn't that remarkable? I have no idea
whether it is true or not. When I questioned her about it, Mother
laughed at first and then she told me, quite seriously, that I must
never mention it again.

In the years since her disappearance, life itself for me has
seemed diminished, its range narrowed, as if a moon had been
shot out of the sky.

Please don't make me think about it anymore.

About your other request, Constantine. I'll have to talk to the
others. They'll agree, probably. But I really don't see what help
I could possibly be in your work. Perhaps if I could see the
documents you're working on.

                                                        MARRA

Letter 4

December 24, 1949

Marra:

I'm leaving this note in the custodian's closet as a last resort. I've already knocked twice at your door, but there's no answer. Felix, the man downstairs, says that the police have been by. I saw Hilda on the fourth floor, but when she saw me, she ran without a word to your flat and locked the door. I can't help you if you don't let me. If you read this, meet me at the coffee house around the corner, say, at seven. If I don't hear from you by then, I'll start taking matters into my own hands. I mean this. Merry Christmas.

[A note in a feminine hand on the reverse side:]

Constantine:

All is well. Well, that's not quite true. They, the police, have absconded with Mother Maria's letters. Foolish of me, I know. There will be more visits unless they can be diverted somehow. We have got a proposal to make — the women in apartment number two. We have discussed it at length. You'll find it very amusing. At the coffee house tonight, nine o'clock.

MARRA

Letter 5

December 27, 1949

Constantine:

How lovely to have been awakened by the Brahms again this morning. The G major sonata, the Adagio movement. My brother played the violin, quite well in fact. Yes, the one who was killed in Silesia. Awful, I'm so conditioned to think in tactical terms that I'm tempted to figure out some way to use that brooding five-note melody as a signal. On second thought, let's leave Brahms out of this, shall we?

Of course, I knew you'd agree to the plan. A man of your ironic temperament could hardly resist an offer from a group of middle-aged nuns to simulate a romance with one of them in order to mislead the police. It's a plot right out of a central European farce — though, perhaps, a tad anticlerical for the operetta crowd.

Joking aside, Constantine, I am pleased, and a little surprised that you're willing to go through with this madness. After all, it places you at least lock-of-hair deep into the line of fire. (You're a deft fellow, though.)

As to the stage directions, we have strict instructions from the playwright: Nothing too intense — just a little hand-holding on the canal and an occasion night-cap at the "Royal" for appearances.

And, Constantine, for the sake of my own vanity, don't be diplomatic: Tell me this complicates your life a little.

MARRA

Letter 6

[no date]

Stanz:

By the way, you needn't bother depositing letters in the custodian's closet any more, I don't think. Given the playscript we have been given for Act Two, scene one, of our little beggar's opera, don't you think we can afford to let people in on the fact that we know each other now? You have got to get your lines down, my friend.

But you're right, eavesdropping is a problem.

That's where I think "Joseph" comes in. Yes, that: whatever it is that you keep referring to as "Joseph." I'm assuming it's a literary project of some sort you have asked me to help you with.

(It is, isn't it, Stanz? I'm not going to open your door some day and find a golem behind your door? "This" [ahem], "my dear, is Joseph.")

Why don't we communicate through him? Leave messages there between the pages....

Letter 7

January 2, 1950

Constantine:

How serious you have become all of a sudden. These studies of yours I suppose. It becomes you, you know, a little sobriety to darken the patina. When you play the piano sometimes one has that sense, too, of something else at work, something capable of extremes.

And the questions you were asking me during our walk on the canal the other day! "What would one make of the statement, 'The whole world was created through repentance'?" That was one of them, wasn't it? Your project, again, yes? But you do have to understand that even we sisters have, for all practical purposes, expunged most religious issues from our conversations. It's just too dangerous to get into the habit of discussing such things out loud. If things were different, perhaps.... Today one can't help fearing a slip during a conversation with neighbors or the baker or the police. Oh, we pray, of course, but ... Perhaps it's that we have been fixed on sheer survival for so long that we have forgotten....

Like I told you, I don't think about the faith any more, Constantine. I think about Hilda and Edith and Ilse. They are old now and Mother's gone. And I think about the police. Your questions about the meaning of repentance: They seemed odd, the words unfamiliar, as if you'd asked me to reflect on a difficult algebraic equation I once did in school. I say this in order to account for my silence.

Constantine, how did you ever manage to get hold of the letters? Hilda said they came in the post last night. We could hardly believe our good fortune. Naturally, we thought we had lost them forever. But the return of Mother Maria's correspondence — there's an element, sir, in the style of the delivery that suggests your involvement. Am I wrong about that? I suppose you spoke to someone. Needless to say, you will deny everything. Daily our debt to you increases, my friend. One wonders if you will ever get your money's worth out of this affair.

I suppose you deserve a small reward, one we sisters can readily grant. These letters are never shown to anyone, though, of course, two of them have coffee stains now — an indication, surely, that security agents have held them to the light, so to speak.

But let me quote this passage from one of them, a text that I'm sure will interest you. You see, Mother Maria spoke often of repentance. In fact, one could probably say that it was her favorite topic. She had a highly personal approach to the issue. You will at least get something out of it, my fine scholar. Perhaps there's something I can do to help you, after all.

[*Excerpt from a letter to the Leipzig house of the Congregation of the Sisters of Our Lady of Nazareth, dated January 1, Feast of the Circumcision of Our Lord, 1938*]

" ... What is the purpose of the Christian life? Why do we pray? Why do we meditate on the Scriptures? Why do we sisters take the three vows of poverty, chastity and obedience? Why give ourselves in humble service?

"Not out of sheer loyalty to a lofty ideal, I hope, still less out of docility. These are thin reeds upon which to rest a house and, should squalls come, they will prove useless to sustain us. Human beings demand motivations that are at least as large as the limits of the imagination.

"No, the purpose of the Christian life is to serve, in all its particular forms, as an instrument that enlarges, not contracts possibilities. Christianity is meant to impart to us a progressively greater capacity for Life, that life which the Apostle Paul daringly characterizes as 'the power which raised Jesus Christ from the dead' (Eph. 1:19) and which in another place he calls 'the power of an indestructible life' (Heb. 7:16).

"And what is the place of sin in this schematic? Sin diffuses our ability to grasp, indeed, finally, even to hope for that life. Sin narrows our focus, withers our human capacities, limits the range and scope of our desires and, ultimately, denies us access to ourselves. Grace breaks into that slumber, to dispel the blindness, and to create capacities for truth, for reality — for life in union with Life.

"There is only one sure way, however, to dispose ourselves to the development of such capacities: the spirituality of repentance.

"And what is repentance? Today, sisters, you must forget your Latin. Repentance is not, in the most important sense, *paenitentia* — sorrow or regret. We shall have to rely on another word and another language in order to recover the concept's ancient splendor.

"*Teshuvah* is the Hebrew word, the Old Testament's word, and it is the meaning of *teshuvah* we must recover. It is best rendered "turning." To repent, then, is to turn: in the religious sense, to turn toward God. That is the focus. By the very nature of that turning to God, we turn away from the darkness. *Teshuvah* means that repentance, first of all, is not about regret, but about choosing to open out one's life.

"The story of the Prodigal Son is instructive in this respect. The prodigal, the Gospel says, 'turned' toward his father. In the very act of 'turning,' he became again the man's son (Luke 15:18), that is, 'he came to his senses' (Luke 15:17) — he realized again who he was, and acted accordingly.

"It is in this light that we live what may rightly be called the culture of repentance: conversion, fasting, penance, prayer, and sacrifice. *Teshuvah* enables us to overcome the fear of suffering (which is the fear of death) and to embrace repentance as the dance of the universe, as the language of Life itself that turns unceasingly toward its source, that is always turning to the Father.

"*Teshuvah* is the key to everything...."

Chapter 6

The Book of Maxims

Introductory Notes
by Constantine Gruber

The Book of Maxims, or *The Thirty-three Maxims of Joseph the Just,* is newly translated from the Faiyumic dialect by Constantine Gruber.[1] By all accounts, Friedrich Schleyer, discoverer of the Joseph Archive, did little more than catalogue this remarkable little collection.

Internal evidence implies that the collection is ascribed to James, or Jacob, the priest, son of Clopas, "brother of the Lord," and leader of the Jerusalem, or Mother, Church, during the age of the apostles. James is, along with apostolic leaders Peter and Paul, a commanding figure in the New Testament, representing, as he does, both the biological family of Jesus and a particularly fervent form of classic Jewish piety in the life of the early Church.

A word about the form of these thirty-three sayings. They have striking similarities with rabbinic literature of the period, particularly with the *Pirkei Aboth* ("Ethics of the Fathers"), a collection of wisdom sayings attributed to the early rabbis and included in the Mishnah of the Talmud.

A case could, of course, be made that the maxims also have resonances with the *Verba Seniorum* or "Words of the Elders" characteristic of the early monastic movement in the Egyptian desert and, hence, the milieu of Mar Yusuf.

Superficially at least, the number of the maxims — thirty-three — would seem to suggest a Christian origin for these sayings. Is not Jesus traditionally supposed to have lived thirty-three years? (There are even Coptic icons of a Christ figure with thirty-three faces — one for each year of his life.)

But while such an explanation is attractive, one also has to remember that the sum is important for other, older, traditions as well. In most Asiatic numerological systems, the number thirty-three represents completion or perfection. In that case, thirty-three maxims would simply imply that what is written here exhausts the known sayings of the sage to whom they are ascribed. And, more importantly, in Jewish tradition, David, the model ruler, is said to

---

1. Faiyumic is one of the five dialects of Coptic (from the Arabic *Gibt,* Egyptian), the native language of Egypt, originating in Pharaonic times and used until the Arab conquest in the seventh century, after which it was gradually replaced by Arabic. The other Coptic dialect used in the Maxims is Bohairic, the dialect of the Nile Delta and Wadi Natrun. —CG.

have reigned thirty-three years — hence, reinforcing the Davidic and Jewish messianic cast of the work.

And then there is always Islam with its ninety-nine "beautiful names" of Allah recited on rosaries of thirty-three beads.

There are other even more compelling reasons why the maxims do not appear to derive from Egyptian monastic circles. The regard they express for the sanctity of the Jerusalem Temple would appear to date them before its destruction in the first century. And those inclined to push for a Coptic, or Egyptian, origin for the sayings will have to explain why monks of Late Antiquity would be preoccupied, as this text is, with the affairs of a Jewish temple by then a memory for two or three hundred years.

Finally, while Jesus is mentioned in several of the sayings, ascriptions of messianic or semi-divine status to him are clearly later interpolations. One can hardly imagine an Egyptian monastic author referring to Christ as "Joshua, son of Joseph," as the author does here. (Except in the later glosses on the text, the Greek form of the name, Jesus, is not employed.)

So, a preliminary assessment would assign these vivid and poignant sayings to a first-century Jewish source, writing or collating his material before the destruction of the Jerusalem Temple by the Roman general Titus in A.D. 70.

Note taped to the back of the first page, undated.

Original, no carbon. Gruber has initialed the note in the upper right-hand corner. Coffee and grease stains are tell-tale signs of considerable rewriting.

How is it my business what Toppler does with his free time? Doubtless, had I been present at what must have been the beer bust to ring down the ages, I would have warned our enthusiastic project chief not to lie to the KGB! How could he have let himself go like that? Don't tell me, Martin. I know.

"The Soviets have been apprised of the importance of your work," he writes. "And they are most eager to see the results. Most eager" — underlined in red. "The *most* important people, you understand."

How could Toppler have gone off and told the KGB that we have got the goods on Jesus' family, the real story in black and white? I know, Martin. It was the Black Sea vodka and the Bavarian ale and the Georgian wine and the fine plum brandy — but they believed him, Martin, they really believed him!

I've taken the phone off the hook twice this week. Toppler calls me in the middle of the night!

When I sent you the text of the maxims of Joseph, I thought it would quiet things down. I thought you would see how sensible it was for me to spend so much time on them, that you would see how remarkable they were. Instead, you give me this line about focusing on the more "productive texts."

You were once more thoughtful, my friend. What's happening to you? Don't tell me. I know...

[*The note breaks off abruptly here. From all indications, it was never sent.* —Ed.]

✍

THE MAXIMS OF REPENTANCE

1. Joseph the Builder, son of Jacob, received this tradition from his fathers, and he said, If the whole people of Israel observed but one day of Atonement, if all the people fasted and repented as God has commanded, but once only, Messiah would come.

2. This saying is not to glorify the Messiah, he explained, but to show the power of repentance.

3. Some Samaritans for whom Joseph was building a house once pointed out a man who was being flogged publicly for some offense. When Joseph heard his cries, he said to the Samaritans, This man weeps [for his sins].[2] If the Holy One were here, he would treat him like a bridegroom.

4. Similarly, he once told Hani, son of Amos, the preacher of Kefar Cana, Never sorrow over the penitent, rejoice with him instead. Give him not tears, but wine and oil and song.

5. To James, the priest, son of Clopas, whom Herod Agrippa had flung into the Kidron, he once said, The number of the Messiah is thirteen, as it is written, "Now the sons of Jacob were

---

2. As before, later monastic glosses are bracketed. —CG.

twelve." The twelve plus one, the one outside the circle, this is the one who will be betrayed, who will break the fastened chain.

6. Also, to James, son of Clopas, Joseph the Builder once said, Do not fear the Roman cross. Do you not know that the spirit of the Holy One was once stretched out upon the waters and that out of his wounds the oceans of repentance were fashioned?

7. He said, Repentance created the world. [By this, he meant God "turning" toward man.] And as salt preserves food, so repentance preserves the world.

8. Joseph the Builder once said in a meeting of the elders of Nazareth, Can a hard man ever be trusted? Like a sealed chest, the treasure of his virtues is useless [even to himself]. Trust only the one who loves repentance.

9. And in a similar vein, he once observed to Hani, the tanner, who had joined a Pharisee brotherhood, A good deed crowned is a good deed destroyed.

10. Enlighten everything, good *and* evil with repentance.

11. On seeing a young farmer plow his field, Joseph the Builder remarked, Open the earth with piety, my son. Is she not your mother and your grave?

12. Similarly, he once said, Wash the earth with your tears and she will not leave your disgrace uncovered [your bones], as did Noah's sons.

Note appended to Maxim 10, written in the hand of Constantine Gruber

Marginal jottings written in Coptic indicate that the monks of Mar Yusuf attached their own legends and traditions to these maxims. There were probably whole collections of these Mar Yusuf stories but only three of them (plus a brief commentary) have come down to us courtesy of these marginalia appearing on leaves four, six, and thirteen of our text. Others may have circulated orally.

The Tale of Brother Mark and the Viper

Marginalia in Bohairic appearing on Leaf 4 of the Book of Maxims.

There was a certain neophyte monk named Mark, afterward called the penitent, who, upon hearing the maxim of our holy father Joseph, thought to go about in the wilderness calling the elements to repent. And so he would stand on one of the low hills and shout to the winds, "Purify yourselves," for he recalled that the holy Joseph had said that the world was created through repentance.

The farmers loved him and bowed low to him as he passed thinking that the monk had magic powers to reconcile the earth to man and, hence, improve the yield of their crops.

But one day, coming upon a viper, Brother Mark stood fearlessly before it and said, "Brother, repent!" whereupon the serpent bit him in the thigh. Repairing to the monastery, the good brother soon swelled up like a water skin. A priest was summoned, the monk was reconciled to all and died.

When the brothers standing by asked an elder why the snake had been permitted to wound him, seeing that the monk had meant him no harm but, rather, sought to bless him and all creatures, the elder replied: "God's creatures are on the path of repentance and even monks, though sinful, are on that same path, but the repentant exist to provoke one another."

Note found between the pages of the translation of the Book of Maxims

A loose note scribbled with a number 2 pencil on a wartime University of Leipzig notepad; the Nazi-period "Victory" stamp is still visible in the upper left-hand corner.

February 22, 1950

Marra:

Well, if it was anyone other than "our Joseph" I'd have been cut to the quick by the remark you made to me last night when we left the "Royal," our neighborhood cafe: "I'm not sure I don't

put up with you only because of him." (By that, I assumed you
meant Joseph.)

Upon reflection, I realized that I deserved that little "Confirmation slap" of yours: I've been a pest about your "Joseph notes,"
haven't I? But Marra, there's a reason. I don't have anyone else
I can turn to with the maxims. Surely you can understand that,
can't you?

I know you understand what's going on.

Tomorrow morning I could walk straight to the rector of the
local Leipzig seminary and ask him what he makes of these
texts — religiously speaking, of course. I can hear it now: "Rev-
erend Father, I'm a linguist working with the State Committee
on Religion and Atheism. (*That* committee, yes.) Can you advise me about the precise character of the religious doctrine in
these apparently ancient epigrams? You know, Monsignor, nothing complicated — just a rough theological profile of the man who
wrote them?"

After the poor man had calculated just how quickly he could
slip into the underground, feeling for a split second the chill of
piano wire against his windpipe, he would be exquisitely polite,
take the copy of the translations and stall, stall, stall for time.

"How interesting, my young friend," he would respond, each
word chewed carefully, slowly, after the manner of some inter-
minable scene in a Russian movie. And then there would be a
catechism-size list of careful, patient inquiries as the man searched
for ways to become the interrogator instead of the interrogatee:
Where had these texts come from? Who do you say discovered
them? Egyptian texts are notoriously unreliable I've heard, so
many forgeries about, and so on.

And who could blame the man for trying to evade the assignment? Who wants to be caught dead, so to speak, responding to
a request from our committee of cursed memory? He would assume we were nosing around for something, looking for some
excuse to make trouble. And, God knows, the good man might be
right. Even I sometimes suspect the committee hasn't the slightest
interest in Joseph and the documents, but that they're....

Enough. You *do* understand.

I need help with the "religious sensibility" side of our Joseph.
Am I sure it's "purely professional," this quest of mine — didn't
you ask me that last night? Well, Marra, once in transit, who

can know all his motives for making the journey? You, above all people, ought to appreciate that.

All I know is that I need your help. So, will you?

CONSTANTINE

March 5, 1950

Marra:

You're avoiding me. What is it?

STANZ

[*Note in a feminine hand on the reverse side:*]

Mr. Gruber:

Stop bothering me, will you? I'm working on it, if for no other reason than I wish to penetrate his secret: Joseph lived in an empire of shadows and yet he was free.

[no signature]

THE TEMPLE MAXIMS

13. Joseph the Builder used to take long walks in the woods with his apprentices in the countryside, looking for choice woods. He said on one of these occasions, The graves of sages and holy men lay all about us unseen. Only the swallows know this secret map of the earth, as it is written: "Where the swallow finds a nest for her brood, your altars, O Lord of hosts. . . . "

14. He had this opinion of the temple which he confided to his son Joshua on entering the Huldah Gates [this was at the time of the pilgrimage to Jerusalem]: Why do the scribes say that the Court of the Gentiles is not holy, but only the place which is beyond the Court of Women? Do not the prophets say that all the nations shall climb the hill of the Lord and worship him in this place together with us?

[This will happen when the King comes.]

15. And Joseph told this story: A Gentile carted his goods each day across the Court of Gentiles because it was the shortest route to his destination. Each day a pious Jew saw him pass and bowed low to him as if he were some religious notable. His friends thought him mad and remonstrated with him: Why do you debase

yourself in front of this dog who uses our temple as a thorough-fare? And the Jew replied: For the sake of the prophets and the seed of holiness [that is in him].

[It was for this reason that Joshua who is called Messiah drove out the moneychangers from the Court of Gentiles before his Passion: to proclaim the holiness of the place and to announce that the time of the ingathering of the nations was at hand.]

16. It was a saying of James, the priest, son of Clopas, who related that Joseph the Builder ate no meat after the bar mitzvah of his son Joshua — that is, except to taste a morsel the size of an olive from the sacrifices prescribed [in the Law]. When asked about this practice, Joseph would say only that if a soldier knows that war is coming, he will prepare himself today.

17. It is true, Joseph said on another occasion about abstinence from meat, that the Lord accepted the meat offerings of Abel, his chosen. But it is right that some should make atonement for Cain, the tiller of the ground.

[All this was in anticipation of the fasting of Christ, who, as it is written in the Gospels, would not eat the meat of the Passover sacrifice before he suffered.]

THE MAXIMS OF HOLINESS

18. And Joseph gave this tradition, that every man has the seed of holiness in him. If one cannot revere him because of his deeds, one is commanded to honor him because of the image that he bears, as it is written, Let us make man in our image and likeness.

19. In this regard, Joseph said that honor waters the seed of holiness.

20. It is like a prince, he said, who, driven mad by the sun, had taken up dressing like a beggar and eating grass. Shouts of alarm and insults served only to enrage him. But there was one wise servant who knew well what to do: She spoke soothingly to him and wooed him into the shade. There she wiped his brow and, ignoring his demeanor, said over and over again, Your Majesty, until he regained his senses.

21. For holiness is within everyone, the holy Joseph said, like a body hidden in the heart of the earth. It is the task of a person's friends to awaken him.

22. It is like a craftsman who has before him a block of wood but knows that there is a graceful bow within it, or a carpenter who holds a branch in his hands, hearing all the while within the murmur of the hidden yoke.

23. That is why when the judge of all takes his seat at the end of the world, he will summon to the tribunal not the sinner only but his companions as well. If the petitioner is wicked, the judge will rend his garments and mourn over the sinner's misspent life. But he will rebuke the friends who failed to unveil the man's [hidden] glory or lift a finger to unbind him.

THE MAXIMS OF THE WOUND

24. James, son of Clopas, related this tradition about Joseph, that the Builder used to say this to his son Joshua: A man never sees clearly until he learns to see out of the wisdom of his wounds, as it is written, Out of his anguish, a man shall see.

25. All human folly consists in this: That a person seeks to flee the world created by what has wounded him.

26. On one occasion, when the Romans had crucified twenty Galileans on the road to Scythopolis, Joseph said to the sons of Clopas: We Jews are born crucified. This is so because God himself was wounded when he created the world. And we are his sons.

But Simon, son of Clopas, responded, Blessed be the Messiah, son of David, who will come without blemish or wound to redeem the children of Israel!

27. Joseph answered him, You do not know what you are saying. The Messiah will be the most wounded one of all.

Marginal note next to Maxim 27

In the Faiyumic dialect. From certain syntactical details, it seems to have been set down quite some time after the Arab conquest of Egypt in the seventh century, perhaps even as late as the ninth century(?). But the trappings of the tale hearken back to a much earlier time.

The Tale of the Tryst

There was a certain young monk named Arsenius who had studied in Alexandria with a great pagan master. Once having joined the brotherhood, however, he never once sought to display his learning in the presence of the monks, but was distinguishable from the other brothers only by the recollection of his spirit.

After several years in the monastery, however, brother Arsenius showed one other singular characteristic: on moonless nights, after the midnight office, he was observed slipping out of the monastery to walk alone into the desert where the hyenas and wild dogs prowl. Before dawn, he would return to his pallet to rise again for morning prayer.

When questioned about his behavior, Arsenius would offer only that he went into the night to bathe his wounds. More he would not say.

As the practice of the perambulations continued, some of the brothers began to suspect him. "He journeys not for some holy purpose," these whispered, "but to tryst with some Bedouin woman unobserved," they said.

So several of the older monks held an official conference with Arsenius's elder, the one to whom the monk confessed. "We know that he leaves the protection of the enclosure on only the darkest nights," they said. "Surely, it is your duty to tell us who it is that beckons him into the wild where danger and temptation lurk."

But the elder would say only, "If you must know, follow him."

So, on the first moonless night, after the midnight office had been sung, a company of senior monks observed the young Arsenius leave the monastery as was his custom, and, fanning across the landscape, pursued him. Their prey did not prove easy quarry. He journeyed deep into the lightless desert, walking for what seemed hours, and, finally, coming upon a low ridge of hills, scaled them with his bare hands.

At the summit, there was a kind of plateau. There the monk sat for a long time on his haunches as if eagerly awaiting a visitor. The elders, hiding in the rocks, strained to see who would join him there.

After a very long time, the monk arose, and drew out a wooden cross from his tunic and placed it on the ground before him. He began to pour out his heart to the unseen presence in a loud voice, confessing there all his doubts in language that would have earned him the name "blasphemer" had it been uttered in a believer's hearing.

For hours, the young monk remonstrated with God — accusing him, begging him, taunting him, weeping over him.

Then the elders knew at last the meaning of his answer to their inquiries: I go into the night to bathe my wounds, and left him to his devotions. For they remembered the words of the holy Joseph who said that a man learns to see out of the wisdom of his wounds.

And Arsenius was credited with the greatest of the customs of the monks [of Mar Yusuf]: that on moonless nights, the monks, moved by grace, may journey into the desert alone to pour out their hearts before God.

The brothers called the custom "the tryst."

THE MAXIMS OF SILENCE

28. Jose, son of Eliezer, the son of Hyrcanus, once delivered this saying of Joseph's to Simon, the brother of James: The tongue is the creator of worlds. As such, it is necessary to compel it to observe the Sabbath. But as for mercy, it is God's drudge: let it work.

29. And the holy Joseph said, Righteousness of the tongue is the highest righteousness. And there is no righteousness of the tongue without silence.

30. Joseph once said this at the close of the Sabbath: And in what does the holiness of the tongue consist? That a person die of love without speaking.

[Of whom did the holy Joseph speak in this saying, Simon once inquired of James. "Of Mary, his wife," was the reply, "the one whom the disciples call the Woman. But do not ask what the maxim means," James added. "There are mysteries about which it is unwise to speak, but this is a mystery about which it is unwise even to think."]

31. Silence is never the mere absence of speech, Joseph once confided to his son Joshua. Silence is as full of sound as a mirror is full of light. A man of silence is the one whose very breath is music, and in the light of whose eyes the heavens open.

32. James, the priest, the son of Clopas, said this about the silence of the holy Joseph: There were three seasons of his silence:
when he heard that Mary, his betrothed, was with child; when
Joshua came of age; and when his son placed coins on his eyes,
that is, when he fell asleep [in a place unknown.]

[This also is the meaning of the three silences of Jesus: when he
was a child; when he went to the mountains to pray; and when he
was silent before his accusers.]

33. [The text here is badly garbled, the document showing
signs of repeated erasures. The only two recognizable words are:
"Nazoreans (Nazarenes)" and "rivers"(?). —CG]

It is possible that the saying was considered heretical. After all,
Jewish-Christians, presumably the source of these traditions, became suspect in later centuries and some of their notions appear in
the lists of the fourth-century Church Father Epiphanius's eighty
heresies.

But the monks of Mar Yusuf had a more ingenious explanation:
The final maxim of Joseph was an invitation to the silence that he
himself embodied. This is contained in the final marginal note the
monks attached to the Book of Maxims.

Final marginal note to the Book of Maxims
In Bohairic. Late sixth century.

And the last word of the Father is silence.

᎒

Excursus on James the Just
by Constantine Gruber

Carbon copy of a typewritten set of notes for project
coordinator Martin Niebel
Date uncertain, but written during the period of Gruber's work on the
maxims.

Okay, so you guys want to know my theories about James. That's
more like it, Martin, like the Martin I used to know, the one whose

principal academic charm was his earnest, positively "Bavarian" sense of history. (The old boy really believes this stuff, the Joseph Archive and its claim to represent the traditions of the family of Christ, I used to say to myself, in the privacy of my own... slipped out, Martin, just slipped out: *private thoughts*. Whatever would our "keepers" make of an elitist phrase like that, eh?)

Sorry. I'm not really trying to get you in trouble. Just happy, that's all. You gentlemen have been behaving lately like a pack of doctoral examiners in linguistics, if I may say so. All these detailed questions about Coptic grammar and usage. It seemed to me that we had forgotten all about Joseph and the propagandistic potential of our little treasure. I can't tell you how reassured I am.

So, on to the presumed "author" of the maxims, James, or Jacob, the Just, the Righteous, "brother of the Lord." (By the way, assure the committee that this is based on solid German scholarship, on Walter Bauer, to be exact. Assure Toppler that I don't rely on French experts for anything serious.)

(How's Julia, by the way? Haven't seen her about for two days. Most inconvenient, Martin. Have you spirited her away?)

1. Paul's epistles and the Acts of the Apostles record a number of important facts about James. He was vouchsafed a separate, that is unique, appearance of the risen Christ (1 Cor. 15:7); he ranked among "the pillars" of the primitive Church in Jerusalem (Gal. 2:9); Acts goes on to clarify that he was its representative and leader (Acts 15:13–22) and one whom the other apostles, including Paul, seek out for advice in disputed questions and whose directives they obey (Acts 21:18–26).

2. Roughly contemporary with these accounts, the Jewish historian Josephus mentions the martyrdom of James (*Antiquities of the Jews*, 20: 9, 1) as part of a power play instigated in the absence of a Roman procurator by the High Priest Ananus the Younger in the middle of the year A.D. 62. The latter summoned James and some others before a council of judges on the charge of having acted against the Law and handed them over for stoning. But many Jerusalem residents objected to the deed and, after protesting to Agrippa and the Roman procurator Albinus, secured the deposition of Ananus from the office of High Priest. The early Alexandrian theologian Origen affirms that a lost Josephus text represents the destruction of the Jewish Temple eight years later

as divine punishment for the execution of James, whose piety was widely admired by Jews and Christians alike.

3. Hegesippius, about the year 180, amplifies this tradition in an extensive "memoir" that influenced the early Church historian Eusebius. The profile of James according to Hegesippius adds the following details:

- James was ritually pure from birth;

- the future leader drank neither wine nor strong drink;

- he also shrank from the razor and, it would seem, the bath, like a Nazirite (for parallels, see Acts 21:23–24);

- he never wore wool, but only linen;

- because of this, he alone was permitted within the temple sanctuary;

- there he prayed night and day on his knees for the people, so that his nickname among the Jews of Jerusalem was "oblias" or "protection (rampart, strong tower) of the people";

- and although he was attacked for a variety of reasons by members of all the Jewish parties of the day, nevertheless, even among their leaders, he had partisans and admirers because of his prestige and blameless observance of the Law.

Hegesippius provides many details about the martyrdom of James, his account having strong overtones of the New Testament's account of the martyrdom of Stephen (Acts 7:54–60).

" '... Why do you ask me with regard to Jesus, the Son of man? He sits in heaven at the right hand of the great Power, and will one day come on the clouds of heaven.' Thereupon the scribes and Pharisees hurled him down into the Kidron Valley, and, since he was still alive, began to stone him. But he prayed on his knees: 'I pray thee, Lord God our father, forgive them, for they know not what they do.' Then a priest ... cried out, 'Stop! The Just is praying for you!' Then one of them, a fuller, took the cudgel he used for beating clothes, and with it struck him on the head; and so James met with a martyr's death."

Interestingly, the event is precipitated in Hegesippius by the urging of "some scribes and Pharisees that he give testimony from the pinnacle of the Temple court as to what was 'the gate [that is, the significance] of Jesus the crucified.'" Hegesippius dates the martyrdom of James to a time later than Josephus's account: the Passover probably of A.D. 66, one of the last universally observed Passover feasts before Vespasian's armies laid siege to Jerusalem in A.D. 70.

4. That James was a widely admired figure among the Jewish people is evident in the Talmud, where in the Tosephta, or "supplements," the young Galilean Rabbi Eliezer ben Hyrcanus finds himself arrested by the Romans as a Christian because he once "approved" of a saying of Jesus told him by one Jacob of Kefar Sikhnin (or Sama), long assumed by scholars to be James, "the Lord's brother." Significantly, the saying of which the rabbi approved had to do with the ritual purity of the Temple. Also important is that the Jacob of Kefar Sikhnin story is told in the context of a discussion of the problem of "uttering charms over a wound," that is, healing in the name of the Messiah.

5. In the Gospel of the Hebrews, cited by many of the early Fathers (Clement of Alexandria, Origen, and Jerome, particularly), James's abstinence is noted in the context of the Last Supper, thus:

> "...James had sworn that he would not eat bread from that hour in which he drank the cup of the Lord until he should see him risen...And shortly thereafter, the [risen] Lord said: Bring a table and bread! And immediately it is added: he took bread, blessed it, broke it, and gave it to James the Just and said to him: My brother, eat thy bread, for the Son of man is risen from among them that sleep."

This, of course, has resonances with the maxims and, indeed, with Conon's History as well, in that Joseph fasted in connection with the revelation of the Messiah.

6. Finally, Eusebius notes the royal authority of James as a Davidic heir, declaring that James's episcopal chair was preserved as a relic in his time and Epiphanius, a Palestinian bishop, concurs, noting that James sat on the throne of David. The good bishop also repeats the tradition that James was, like the High Priest, permitted to enter the Holy of Holies once a year.

7. All this, taken together, gives us the impression, not only

that James was a saint, but hints, through a maze of enigmatic assertions, that James may well have functioned as a quite public person in the last days of the Second Temple Period.

Clearly James has something to do with the Jewish Temple. While the business of entering the Holy of Holies — an act unthinkable to anyone but the High Priest — is attributed to his extraordinary piety, there's another, more obvious possibility. Perhaps James actually served, however briefly, as high priest of the Jerusalem Temple. This places the enmity of Ananus in perspective and gives Josephus's remark about the martyrdom of James and the destruction of the Temple more point. Later on, the culturally Gentile Church, in growing antipathy to the synagogue, would find it inconvenient to remember this part of the story.

In any case, James stands as the last in the "Josephite" line, a just or righteous one, a member of the royal house of David, and, in a sense, more the Builder's spiritual "heir" than Joshua, his only son, who went on to have quite a different sort of career. In any case, James is the sort of tragic figure, full of serenity, one finds only at the end of an age: the last emperor of Byzantium.

᭡

Editor's Notes

It is at this point that we find the first of thirteen odd jottings or numerological designs scribbled on the reverse side of page 3 of Gruber's notes on the maxims: four unequal sets of consecutive numbers in four uneven rows written in blue-black ink. In addition, there are two sets of numbers in red ink inserted in rows 2 and 4 respectively. Thus:

[blue] 1 2 3 4 5   6 7 8

[red] 9 10 11 12 [blue] 13 14 15

[blue] 16 17 18 19

[red] 20 21 22 23

The careful penmanship suggests that the puzzle is to be taken seriously. —Ed.

Chapter 7

The Passion of Joseph the Just

Notes by Friedrich Schleyer

It is not without reason that one of the medieval scholars of Mar Yusuf likened this work to a "winding sheet" [marginal notation 1(a) — CG]. Of all the texts of the Joseph Archive, it is the most fragmentary. In fact, it reads more like an anthology of traditions about Joseph's passing than a standard narrative.

The text as we have it seems to have been adapted by the monks of Mar Yusuf as a liturgical text for their celebration of Joseph's death, the Feast of the Bath, observed annually on the day after the Dormition, or Falling Asleep of the Virgin, on August 16. (It may also have been employed as a funerary text.) Given our present state of knowledge, it is not possible to disentangle and date with any precision the various [liturgical and literary] strands that go to make up the tapestry.

Like all the works that make up the Joseph Archive, a mystery stands at the heart of the *Passion:* in this case, the matter of a missing grave. The text scrupulously avoids the subject of the circumstances under which Joseph was buried. And there is no early tradition for a burial site in the Holy Land, either. Egypt, so far as we can determine, does not become a dubious candidate for the honor until late in the Monophysite controversies of the sixth century.

Perhaps the lapse may be due to the fact that much early Christian tradition saw Joseph as too ambiguous a figure — not the sort to honor with a vivid public cult. We have only to take a cursory glance at the various apocryphal gospels to see that Joseph was viewed in those documents at worst as a kind of sacred cuckold or, at best, a character out of a particularly cruel, if poignant, form of domestic comedy. But one has to wonder about the business of the grave and, more importantly, what its absence suggests. —FS

Addendum by Constantine Gruber

Actually, Schleyer was not quite right about the Holy Land end of his musings. The medieval Russian abbot Daniel mentions seeing a tomb of Joseph in Nazareth in 1107 near the Church of the Annunciation. Fifteenth-century Dominican Felix Fabre locates Joseph's tomb near the tomb of Absalom in Jerusalem's Kidron

Valley. Later pilgrims mention it as a chapel in nearby Gethsemane or in the Church of the Assumption. As a result of excavations in 1909, the convent of the Dames de Nazareth boasts today an ancient tomb that they have identified as the tomb of Joseph. However, all these designations are extremely late and, hence, unreliable. Schleyer's point remains: there is no early tradition on the whereabouts of Joseph's tomb.

If one is required, however, there is always the Egyptian version of events. In a late-vintage legend, it is claimed that Joseph was buried at a site near Taposiris outside Alexandria. (A medieval period account, however, which can be viewed at the monastery of St. Menas fails to mention precisely how he got there.) What we have in the Taposiris tale would seem to be less a piece of historical speculation than a species of wordplay on the fact that Joseph the Builder has the same name as the biblical patriarch Joseph whose body was buried in Egypt to await the deliverance of Israel.

> "Then Joseph said to his brothers, 'I am about to die; but God will surely come to you and bring you up out of this land to the land that he swore to Abraham, to Isaac, and to Jacob.' So Joseph made the Israelites swear, saying, 'When God comes to you, you shall carry up my bones from here.' "
>
> [Gen. 50:24–25]

In any case, we have no clear literary attestation of the story until the Byzantines destroyed the Taposiris tomb during one of several attempts to suppress anti-Chalcedonian sentiment in Alexandria.[1]

The story is that the Byzantines thought the tomb contained the bones of a Monophysite bishop, also called Joseph, whom they imagined the monks of Taposiris honored. (The bones found there were ground to powder and mixed with the fodder of the army's pack animals.) After this incident the claim of the Taposiris monks that they honor the grave of Joseph, father of the Savior

---

1. Monophysite controversy: major theological-cultural split that developed in the wake of the Council of Chalcedon (A.D. 451) between the Oriental churches (Egypt, Syria, Ethiopia, Armenia) on the one hand, and imperial Christianity (Constantinople, Rome) on the other. The first great rift in Christianity, the Monophysite, or better, anti-Chalcedonian revolt, focused not only on theological issues, (i.e., the proper philosophical vocabulary with which to describe the union of human and divine natures in Christ), but linguistic and cultural ones as well (i.e., the difficulty of translating Greek and Latin terms into Syriac and Coptic and age-old Oriental resistance to imperial domination). —CG

in the flesh, begins to grow. The site was not fully restored until the Middle Ages. Much later, a Russian count acquired the site in 1872 as part of the repayment of a drunken wager. Determined to demonstrate his piety, the count made preparations to build a splendid church above the simple Islamic-style cenotaph, now exposed to the elements. Funds ran out six years later, however, with the result that the site today remains open to the sky but graced with an impressive free-standing west facade done in the best St. Petersburg style, slowly sinking into the soft Delta ooze. —CG

1. HOW JESUS TAUGHT HIS DISCIPLES ABOUT THE PASSING OF JOSEPH

In the days before his passion, Joshua imparted the "secret teaching" — that is, the teaching that can be passed only by word of mouth — to the disciples on the Mount of Olives, as it is written: "While he was seated on the Mount of Olives — that is, seated like a rabbi, facing the temple — his disciples came to him privately — that is, without the multitude — and said: What will be the sign of your coming and the end of the world? And Jesus began this discourse . . . "[2]

And in another place, it is written: "He would teach in the temple by day and leave the city to spend the night on the Mount of Olives — that is, to spend the night in teaching the things that are veiled."[3]

[This place is known to us today as the Church of Mercy, or Eleona, the very same place of which it is said that the Lord will return there on the clouds of heaven to judge the living and the dead.]

There in the Cave of the Teaching, the Master, one by one, revealed all the mysteries there are to the disciples.

[This is why there are many convents today in the vicinity of the Mount of Olives: to live day and night in the light of the mysteries that were communicated there.][4]

---

2. Matt. 24:3, Mark 13:5. —FS
3. Luke 21:37. —FS
4. The Church of the Eleona (Church of the Olives) was founded by Helena, mother of Constantine, in the fourth century on the Mount of Olives, which subsequently be-

And he told them how it happened, the going forth from the body of our father Joseph the Builder, father of Messiah according to the flesh.

[This account was once given by the cohen Jacob, James, the priest, bishop of Jerusalem to the council of the Davidic priests of Bethlehem, in accordance with the custom that the words and portents associated with the passing of one of David's line be set down in writing.]

૭

And when Joseph reached the age when craftsmen turn over their work to their sons, Joseph, too, was prevailed upon by his son Joshua and the sons of Clopas to take his rest.

But when it came to repairs, Joseph was adamant.

"If something is amiss in the work," he would say, "it is up to the workman himself to make it right — though it is the matter of the straightening of a single brick." And he could never be persuaded to accept the smallest payment for repairs.

"In the eye of the Almighty, the world is already perfect," he told his workers, "but does he not, nevertheless, labor like a slave night and day to perfect it?"

On one occasion, Joseph's eye failed him when he tried to align a course of stone precisely. "The task," he said to his workers, "is to see the wall from God's angle. But I, as you see, am a mere penitent." With a smile, he ceded the task to Joshua, his son, who saw the problem at once and corrected it.

So Joseph let his son and the apprentices take on the larger construction projects, contenting himself with the repair work.

With his son attending to business, Joseph could at last afford to spend his mornings in the House of Studies in Sepphoris. The provincial capital was a mere three miles' walk from Nazareth and was equipped with the best library in Galilee, that is, until more than half of its scrolls were carted away to Tiberias on the Sea of Galilee when the seat of government was moved there after the Builder's death.

What did the Builder study in Sepphoris?

---

came a major center of spirituality in Byzantine times, with, historians report, more than two dozen convents and monasteries on its slopes. These foundations and their inhabitants were wiped out with gruesome efficiency by the Persians in 614. The Coptic transcriber here has confused the Greek word *eleion* (olive) with *eleios* (mercy). —FS

In the synagogue, the Builder, as one would expect, was able to meditate on the Torah and to consult the views of scholars when problems of interpretation arose. Menelaus, who was a member of the Builder's study group, related to James, the priest, that, outside the usual study of the scriptural portion for the week, Joseph spent a great deal of his time in Sepphoris examining the texts and asking questions about his namesake, the patriarch Joseph, the visionary, who was Pharaoh's vizier in Egypt.

Menelaus reminisced that it was easy to know what Joseph studied since his voice was distinctive and he always studied out loud.

Menelaus also claimed that the Builder made use of the Roman library situated near the barracks in Sepphoris. Not that the craftsman had more than a rudimentary grasp of Latin, but he sought to examine the large collection of drawings housed there on the public buildings of Rome.

The Builder's afternoons were always spent at home with Miriam, helping her with her work. Joseph and Miriam would sit for hours in the shade of the fig tree Joshua had planted as a boy in their courtyard, stringing dried mint or preparing yoghurt or repairing the jars for food storage.

And all Nazareth marvelled at Joseph's love for Miriam, his wife. No one had ever heard him so much as speak sharply to her — and Nazarenes are known for the vividness of their speech, and Nazareth men, particularly, for their harshness. The Builder rose always when his wife approached like one would for a daughter of David the King — more than a few Sabbath guests had told of such things.

But not all were appreciative of such virtues. "What, will my wife expect me now to start stringing garlic with the women too?" some of the men said to one another.

Nazarene women, however, were scarcely less critical. They had long gossiped about Joseph's way with Miriam. In fact, they had pinned a cruel nickname on her, a name that she was sometimes made to overhear when she went to fetch water at the village spring — "Make way for Bathsheba!"[5]

---

5. The epithet refers to the adulterous wife of Uriah the Hittite, later the wife of King David and mother of King Solomon (2 Sam. 11:1–12:25). —FS

2. THE MEAL WITH THE ANGEL
OF THE COUNCIL

On the day of the accident, an angel [messenger] from the council of the priests in Bethlehem paid Joseph a visit. It had been a very long time since the Builder had had direct dealings with the council. There had been courtesy calls, of course, and the occasional small wax imprint of the six-pointed Bethlehem star — the family's insignia — found at building sites — reminders of the family's abiding interest in his activities. But the last time there had been extensive discussions had been in connection with Joshua's council interview, when the family went to Jerusalem for the feast, when Joshua had dazzled the priests with his questions.

For reasons that escaped the others at the time, Miriam seemed particularly apprehensive about the messenger's visit. So much so that she sent Simon, the son of Clopas, to summon Joshua from his work at Kefar Cana.

Pulling Simon aside, out of the hearing of the others, she said, "Tell Joshua to return home at once. It is his mother who speaks. He is needed at his father's side."

So Simon excused himself from the meal that Miriam and her sisters were hastily setting out in the house and went to find Joshua and James, who were preparing to start construction nearby on a new dressing quarters for the synagogue mikveh [ritual bath].

What frightened the mother of Joshua about the visit of the angel?

The Master related three things to the disciples on the Mount of Olives that had inspired his mother's fears: the suddenness of the messenger's appearance, that the angel communicated no message from the council, and that the sleeve of his garment was torn as if in mourning.

To add to the peculiarity of the occasion, the angel said little during the meal, even in the way of news, and ate only a single morsel from each of the dishes that were offered to him. And he touched not a drop of wine.

3. THE SUMMONS OF THE LINTEL

In the midst of the meal with the angel, a boy came from the house of one Eliahu, called the Leper by locals after a skin condition that plagued him. This Eliahu was a tradesman who had bought a farm just over the Nazareth ridge, on the other side of the mountain called the Guard [of the Esdraelon Valley].[6]

The servant announced in the presence of the company that Joseph's help was urgently needed at Eliahu's estate, where Joseph had some time ago built an elaborate stone facade to grace a doorway. So it seemed, the earth underneath the doorway had shifted during the night, causing one of the door jambs to totter, threatening the lintel itself. A whole section of the structure was in danger of collapse.

"Come," said Joseph, rising from his place. And he prepared to go with the boy immediately.

But Miriam, full of foreboding, begged the Builder to remain until Joshua could come from Kefar Cana to assist him.

"Calamities do not wait," the Builder replied with a smile. "When Joshua arrives, tell him where to find me." And taking a wreath of acanthus leaves mixed with anemones he had woven early that morning to surprise her, Joseph placed it on Miriam's brow.

His hand descended to meet her cheek.

"Do not be afraid, mother of Joshua," he said in a quiet voice that belied the feeling within it.

And grasping his walking staff, he apologized to his guests and followed Eliahu the Leper's servant out of the house.

As for Miriam, she stood in the road for a long time bedecked with her crown and watched Joseph climb the ridge until the mountain took him from her sight.

4. WHAT JOSHUA SAID WHEN HE SAW THE SWALLOWS

It wasn't until the last hours of sunlight that Joshua, summoned from Kefar Cana, was found racing up the path called the Three

---

6. The name Nazareth itself, while uncertain, probably means "to guard." —CG

Poplars toward the dark ridge of the Nazareth Mountains in the direction of Eliahu the Leper's estate. Simon was just behind him, his legs already heavy with fatigue.

At the first word of the message Simon brought from his mother, Joshua had dropped his tools on the spot and, leaving James to apologize to the synagogue beadle, had started running back to Nazareth. At the crossroads on the edge of town, he found Simon's brother Judas waiting for him. "Your father's already gone to the house of Eliahu the Leper," Judas shouted, pointing up the ridge. "Hurry!"

Just then Joshua saw a flock of swallows scatter in the sky above the ridge.

"Blessed are you, O Lord, our God, King of the Universe," Joshua said, lowering his head, "the true judge."

"What are you saying, Joshua, son of Joseph," Judas cried. "Your father has need of you. Why utter the blessing on hearing evil tidings?"

"Do you not see flocks of swallows scattering across the sky like dark lightning?" Joshua replied, his features tensing. "They do that only when the arm of the Holy One has fallen."

5. THE THREE MESSENGERS

And Judas joined Joshua and Simon in the search for the Builder's whereabouts. But Joshua outran them all, leaping up the slope like a young ram.

Near the place of the Three Poplars, a messenger from Eliahu met them, saying, "Joshua, come quickly!"

"What is amiss?" said Joshua evenly. "Is my father well?"

"I do not know," the messenger replied. "I know only that I was sent by my master to fetch you at a runner's pace!"

A second messenger met them further up the road.

"Joshua, son of Joseph, there has been an accident at the house of Eliahu the Leper!" he cried.

"Is my father well?" Joshua demanded.

"There's not a moment to lose," the servant shouted, turning to scramble up the final stretch of hillside.

At the place of the Three Poplars, at the top of the ridge, from which the two great valleys can be seen — the Esdraelon and the

Jezreel — where the traders pass on the last leg of their journey to Sepphoris, a third messenger awaited.

"Joshua," he said gently, grasping his shoulders. "Wait now. Your father comes!"

6. THE FRINGES OF JOSHUA'S GARMENT

Farmhands from the house of Eliahu crossed the toll road, bearing the body of the Builder on their shoulders. It already had all the markings of a funeral. The Builder's fulsome cloak was wrapped about him like a shroud. The master of the house, Eliahu the Leper, led the proceedings, his rash-splotched face covered against the ill effects of the air by a veil of black silk.

There was no time for explanations. Joseph was still breathing, but his face was immobile as a mask. Joshua was informed by Eliahu, amid repeated apologies, that his father could not speak.

As Joshua leaned over the face of Joseph, he saw in the still gray eyes an expression he had never seen before. "From this," it seemed to say, "even you cannot shield me."

The breezes of early twilight swept Joshua's *tzitzit*[7] over the countenance of Joseph.

Joshua felt the slightest of tugs at his side. It was his father's hand. He had grasped hold of one of the sacred fringes and was holding on for dear life.

"You see," Joshua said, his voice husky with tears, "even now this man clings to Torah!" [Another would similarly cling to the fringe of Joshua's cloak in the days of his disciples — the woman with an issue of blood, and she was healed of her condition. But because the day of his revelation was still some way off, the power was restrained.[8]]

And so Joshua walked beside his father as they bore him into the village, the holy fringe from his garment firmly wound between the Builder's fingers.

---

7. The sacred fringes attached by immemorial tradition to the four corners of the garment of Jewish males. The fringes symbolize the mitzvot, or commandments, enjoined by God on Israel. —CG

8. See Matt. 9:20. —FS

7. HOW JOSEPH STOOD IN THE BREACH

Later that evening, Eliahu the Leper related what had occurred.

"I blame myself for everything that has happened," the rich man said. "Your father warned me that the ground beneath the eastern wing of my house was too soft to support the great carved doorway I had envisioned. But I insisted, telling him that if he should agree to attempt it, I would donate a large sum of money for the poor of Jerusalem that he could take with him to the Holy City on the next pilgrimage.

"You know the trouble I've had with the local people," he went on. "How they abuse me, throw stones and shout 'leper, leper' after me. I wanted to hurl their ridicule back in their faces, do something that would drive them wild with envy. But instead of silencing my enemies, pride, like a serpent, has wounded the friend who stood at my side."

"Tell us everything," Joshua said to him quietly. "We hold nothing against you."

"When your father arrived," Eliahu went on, "he saw at once that the slippage was serious and that the stonework was in imminent danger of collapsing. He ordered one of my servants to bring as many oak logs as he could find while the Builder knelt in the doorway with a woolen string determining the angle at which they would need to be positioned to keep the lintel from falling. It all happened so quickly.

"Without warning," he continued, "the lintel fell — a solid piece of stone, cut by the Builder's own hand. Your father was standing directly beneath it when it fell. The full weight of the doorway collapsed upon him. An ordinary man's back would have crumbled on the spot. But I tell you, Joshua, son of Joseph, your father was like Samson, supporting the gate with his own strength, his arms outstretched, head lowered, his back spread wide like the wings of an eagle.

"He did not cry out or curse. He was utterly silent, focused, holding up all that stone — just as if he were holding up a universe. Servants rushed to him, of course, one pulling a large oak log which they finally managed to lodge into place behind him. With the lintel supported, they were at last able to free him from his predicament.

"But, alas, my friends, when they released him, the Builder

himself collapsed before us. Like a bursting waterskin, he fell face-first to the ground. And when we turned him over, the only thing which he could move was his mouth. He kept trying to say something."

At this, the angel of the council stepped forward. "And were you able to discern his words?" he asked, looking directly into the estate owner's face with an intensity that unnerved him. "This is very important to us."

"Yes," Eliahu the Leper replied. "My servants and I were able to make out something, though not very clearly."

"And what was it you were able to make out?" the angel pressed. "The exact words, if you can."

"It didn't make much sense to us, like gibberish," the leper said. "But what the Builder was trying to hiss through his teeth were the words:

> "The door,
> the door is open
> now."

8. WHAT JOSHUA SANG TO HIS FATHER
AS HE LAY DYING

Joseph lingered for three days and three nights between earth and heaven — sealed in silence to the last.

Joshua and the women laid him on his mat swaddled in rugs with pots of embers at the four corners to keep him warm. And they placed large black pots of steaming herbs nearby to revive him: rue, hyssop, chamomile, and myrrh.

Joshua and James bathed him in warm water and rubbed him down in the morning and evening with fragrant Judean oils. Seeing that the man could not manage to swallow more than few drops of the broths prepared for him, Miriam massaged his throat every hour and placed moistened cloths on his lips.

As for Joseph, his body seemed to slowly transform itself hour by hour into a vessel of light, as if lit from within. Where there had once been a face full of warmth and color, now there was a skin as translucent as glass. His hair, once sun-burnished a golden-gray, now seemed white as an albino's. Even his eyes seemed drained of color.

When a villager asked if the Builder still "slept," Miriam responded, "My husband does not sleep, he burns."

Visitors to the sick man's house observed that Joshua kept constant vigil, seated at Joseph's head, while Miriam never moved from her position at her husband's feet.

And all the while, day and night, Joshua sang the Song of Songs to comfort him, that poem of Solomon's in which all the secrets of the universe lay hidden.

He murmured its phrases gently in the man's ear, repeating over and over again the passage describing the beauty of the beloved (which is a catalogue of the delights of the Temple):

> " . . . His head is the finest gold;
> his arms are rounded jewels.
> His body is ivory work,
> encrusted with sapphires.
> His legs are alabaster columns
> set upon bases of gold.
> His appearance is like Lebanon,
> choice as the cedars."[9]

[He did this not only to comfort the Builder but to keep death at bay. Joshua had felt him enter the room and take up his position south of the door. Miriam also sensed this, but said nothing.]

9. WHAT JOSHUA DID WHEN THE ANGEL PAID HIM HOMAGE

The angel of the council also kept vigil at the dying Builder's side.

On the morning of the third day, when the messenger knew that the Builder was about to expire, he went over to Joshua and whispering in his ear the royal greeting, took his hand and kissed it.

But Joshua, incensed, removed his hand from the priest of the council and said in a loud voice: "The son of David lives!"

Whereupon the angel bowed low to him and left the house.

---

9. Song of Songs 5:11, 14–15. —FS

10. THE PRAYER OF JOSEPH

No sooner had the messenger left than the family observed that Miriam placed her head between the feet of her husband, pressing her cheek against the sole of his foot. And Joshua stopped singing suddenly, in the middle of a word.

Silence filled the room.

Joshua took his place at the head of Joseph's mat, but not before he had shot an angry glance in the direction of an unseen presence near the door.

"Not yet," he said, holding up his hand. "He himself will summon you."

And the Builder, his face glistening with oil, opened his mouth wide as if fresh water were about to be poured down his throat. And Joshua, his face streaked with tears, cast his eyes to the ceiling and began to pray the prayer his father could not voice, the prayer he had been assembling out of his silence during the days he lay wounded, the last prayer of Joseph the Just.

[Note: *As we have come to expect from the Mar Yusuf documents, the editors do not furnish us with the text of the great prayer. It was probably considered too sacred to be written down or even rendered in a disguised way or through some sort of cryptogram. Perhaps the prayer was communicated orally to the Mar Yusuf brotherhood. But a marginal note gives us a clue to its transmission:*

"The brothers will listen for it and they will hear."

This would seem to indicate that the monks of Mar Yusuf were encouraged to regard the prayer of Joseph as the fruit of meditation.

Two phrases however appear drawn in red ink below the text of the narrative and may suggest at least the gist of the prayer. The phrases are: "breach the wall of division" and "occupying the borderlands." What such phrases mean is anyone's guess. —CG]

As Joshua spoke the words of the prayer, wind gusts blew up outside, the sudden windstorms that are part and parcel of the Galilean summer when the westerlies descend through the valleys with great speed, stirring up clouds of dust and tearing the boughs off trees.

The strong driving wind roared above the room where Joseph lay as if it were about to pull the roof apart. Lamps sputtered. Grape arbors rattled. Ripped-off branches scraped at the walls.

And then as quickly as it had come, the windstorm ceased.

When the family, huddling together in the shadows, looked up, they saw Miriam kiss the feet of her husband. "They are cold now," she said to her son in a voice that trembled like a poplar.

Joshua nodded slowly at these words and, pushing himself off the ground, held up his left arm and pulled at the sleeve until he had ripped it from end to end.

11. HOW JAMES WAS ANGERED AT THE WASHING

When evening had come, Joseph's body was laid out for the washing.

James [the one who would become a priest, the martyr of the Church of Jerusalem] came forward to assist Joshua with the task. (James was disconsolate, seeing that he had loved the Builder more than any man on earth.)

But placing a hand upon his cousin's shoulder, Joshua informed him that he must perform the washing alone: No one — not even James — might be with him when he dressed his father for the grave.

Joshua therefore performed the ritual of tohorah [anointing] according to the customs of Judea and of the family of David, anointing the ten parts of the body in a line, thus:

the head,
the forehead,
the eyes,
the ears,
the nose,
the mouth,
the heart,
the navel,
the thighs
and the feet.[10]

---

10. The monks of St. Menas claim that this ceremony of anointing was also employed at Mar Yusuf. —CG

At this, James became angry and a rift grew up between the two contractors, Joshua and James, a rift that would be healed only at Joshua's death.

Miriam, hearing of the dispute, went to James and tried to reason with him. "Son," she said, "let it be. It is the ceremony for the death of kings." But the younger man, perceiving himself to be dishonored, refused to be consoled. And his brothers also joined in his anger.

"Has Joshua alone David's blood in his veins?" they said.

[In part, it is for this reason that Joshua's family opposed him when he began to preach in the towns and villages of Galilee.]

12. HOW THE NAZARENES WERE SCANDALIZED BY WHAT THEY SAW

After the washing had been completed, Joseph's body was bound according to the practice of the family of David — that is, with the triangular canopy and the royal seals — and laid out in the courtyard of the house.

[The body was not embalmed as the Egyptians do, nor were any spices packed with the body. Nevertheless, the flesh of the Builder did not undergo corruption but had a fragrance like a cargo of eaglewood.]

(The angel of the council directed the proceedings. It was, in fact, for this very reason that he had journeyed to Nazareth, sent by the priests of the council on the basis of the reading of certain signs.)

And, with the family gathered at the four corners of the courtyard, Joshua sat at the body's head with Miriam seated at the feet. Six lamps were set in the earth to the right and left of the body for the twelve tribes of Israel and a single lamp at the head, representing the messiah.

But when the villagers who came to pay their respects to the Builder saw him laid out in such splendor, in the Egyptian style, wrapped in a golden shroud and blanketed by a white garment marked with the insignia of David — that is, with the royal star — they were scandalized.

"What foolishness!" they said. "Are these 'sons of David' not Jews like the rest of us?" And, upon hearing the reports, many

Nazarenes refused to sit with the family, hurling epithets at them in the street instead.

"Magicians," was what they called them.

13. HOW JOSHUA ANSWERED THE NAZARENES

The family decided that, given the temper of the village, the burial should be performed [quietly].[11]

But Joshua one day, after the seven days of mourning had been concluded, had occasion to pass by the village well. A woman there spoke against the name of his father, imagining that the son did not hear her.

But Joshua turned around and, seizing a water jar, filled it to the brim. He lifted up the vessel for all to see.

"Nazareth!" he shouted, spilling the water on the ground before them, "the Builder came among you like pure water. But you, you would not drink!"

And from that day on, the villagers were tireless in abusing him.

As for Joshua, he was soon warned that Herod's officials in Sepphoris had gotten wind of the "royalist character" of the Builder's wake. So, after discussing the matter with Miriam, he made arrangements to absent himself for a time in Egypt.

Note on the Shrine of St. Menas by Constantine Gruber

A forest green file folder with the tag: ST. MENAS. Pencil on "Balkan Express," Leipzig, freight section stationery; undated.

[*Note:* It is a remarkably slender file, Gruber's dossier on St. Menas, an ancient monastic complex near Alexandria. And yet we know from internal evidence that Gruber began corresponding

---

11. The Coptic word employed here is very rarely used and it is notoriously difficult to translate. It can either mean "quietly" as in "secretly" or, in some ancient manuscripts, the word implies "by a hidden route." This ambiguity reflects — and may also have occasioned — some of the later legends of Joseph's burial in Egypt. —CG

with Abba Pachom of that monastery at least by the summer of 1951, if not earlier, and that those exchanges were a significant, if not decisive, element in all that was to transpire later on. The file, as it now stands, contains only a single letter, mostly on religious questions, and a few file-card odds and ends. —Ed.]

Saint Menas (d. 296) is an unlikely inspiration for an entire Christian culture, but that is what the martyr was. Gruesomely mistreated in the reign of the emperor Maximian, Menas was privileged to have the soles of his feet torn off, his eyes gouged, and his tongue torn out at the roots for Christ. Nevertheless, the saint still managed to deliver an impassioned sermon to his persecutors. Understandably piqued by such obstinacy, the emperor himself delivered the fatal blow and fed the martyr's body to the sea in an iron coffin.

Washing ashore on an Alexandria beach, the casket was carted off for unknown reasons by Bedouin who were shortly plagued by more than obstinate martyrs — a camel that refused to move. Impatient souls, the desert traders proposed to cut their losses and buried their man, coffin and all, in the sands at the border between the desert and fertile land. The burial, however, provided the seed for one of the ancient world's most intriguing spiritual civilizations. Widely hailed as a place of healing because of its limestone springs, a virtual Christian metropolis sprung up at St. Menas between the fifth and seventh centuries.

The local pottery interests saw to it that the healing waters were transported to the Christian world. So great was the cult's popularity that British novelist E. M. Forster, with justice, calls Menas "the god of the Libyan desert."

By the late medieval period, however, nearly all traces of Menas's city had vanished. Earlier descriptions of its architectural marvels and fertile vineyards wax with such wonder that later historians, deprived of hard evidence, were inclined to view the whole business as a species of Christian "Shangri-la" until the ruins of St. Menas were identified in the early twentieth century by the German archaeologist Kaufmann.

Today, Coptic authorities, with little success, are attempting to reclaim the site.

[*Note:* On the reverse side, we find again one of Gruber's puzzles:

1 2 3 4 5   6 7 8

(ha) N Z R M   13 14 15

16 17 18 19

(20) N H R

In the upper left-hand corner, in Gruber's scrawl: "The cryptogram only works in Aramaic." —Ed.]

**Carbon copy of a letter from Constantine Gruber
to Abba Pachom, Monastery of St. Menas at Taposiris**
Paperclipped to the above note.

Leipzig
August 16, 1951

Abba:

Forgive me for writing you so soon, only a matter of weeks after my last letter about the text of the "Prayer of Joseph." Father, I do understand, I assure you, that "I must find the text of the prayer within." Advice worthy of a true Josephite, I might add.

But given the fact that the fast of Our Lady's feast has passed, the Assumption fast, and you are again permitted to receive mail, I can only hope that you will not disdain further inquiries on this matter.

I am only a scholar, after all. I can't be expected to "draw from within" so easily. As a scholar, I am one who loves surfaces, a blind man whispering over braille.

Thank you for your gracious note, by the way, on receipt of the considerable bundle of Coptic carbons of the Joseph Archive and my poor translations. I wasn't sure you would ever get them out there in your Alexandrian wilderness. You didn't tell me if you had anyone there who could read German. I've almost finished reviewing, correcting, and updating Schleyer's work — with the exception of these maddening puzzles that remain: the Prayer of Joseph, as you can imagine, is high on that list.

Let us take this one phrase at a time. Did you not say that the given phrases of the prayer are like two doors, the outer and the inner entrances to the "Gospel of Joseph"? (The characterization is yours.)

All right, then. Here are my questions. Does "breaching the wall of division" — the first phrase — not preserve echoes of the Jerusalem Temple's separation of Jews and Gentiles, a division the Hebrew prophets proclaimed would be set aside in the messianic age?

I'm referring here to the stone barrier that enclosed the entire area of the Temple proper and that blocked the access of non-Jews to the sacred precincts.

Paul's Letter to the Ephesians alludes to this:

> "So then remember that at one time you Gentiles by birth
> ... remember that you were at that time without Christ, be-
> ing aliens to the commonwealth of Israel and strangers to the
> covenants of promise.... But now in Christ, you who were
> once far-off have been brought near by the blood of Christ.
> For he is our peace; in his flesh he has made both groups
> into one and has broken down the dividing wall, that is, the
> hostility between us." [Eph. 2:11–22]

Christianity, then, sees in the symbol of the breaking of the Temple's "wall of hostility," the end of the essential separation of Jew and Gentile in the messianic community, does it not? A point anticipated, not incidentally, in the so-called temple maxims of Joseph [Maxims 13–17] and particularly for our purposes the first three of that group.

Isn't it true that the union of Jewish and Gentile worlds is another way of positing the overcoming of all human divisions in Christ? And that precisely as the prophets had envisioned it, in the gathering of the whole world to worship in the Temple court:

> "And the foreigners who join themselves to the Lord,
> to minister to him, to love the name of the Lord,
> and to be his servants...
> these I will bring to my holy mountain
> and make them joyful in my house of prayer;
> their burnt offerings and their sacrifices
> will be accepted on my altar;

for my house shall be called a house of prayer
for all peoples." [Isa. 56:6–8]

So, then, Joseph's prayer would utter that hope from "the
throne position" (the phrase is yours), that is, with authority: toward Israel on the one hand by means of the promises to David,
and toward the nations by way of the universal spiritual mandate
attributed to the messiah.

I'm just trying to understand the sense of the prayer. (I know
you will tell me to excavate inwardly for answers, but even ex-
cavators have got to know if they are digging in the right place,
don't they?)

As for the second, more enigmatic phrase: "occupying the
borderlands" — you wrote last summer, in the very first of our
letters, that you think this refers principally to the legend of the
Builder's burial in Egypt: "borderlands," as in lands outside the
Land of Israel. But surely there has to be more to these words than
a mere confirmation of the Taposiris legend.

Let me try these interpretations out on you.

"Occupying the borderlands" — could the phrase refer to a
vocation to live in permanent contradiction? (The phrase is not
mine, it is my assistant, Marra's, the one I told you about.)
Could it be that the Josephite view of Christianity was that of a
community living on the edges of all earthly and heavenly divisions: to anticipate, in some way, and to point toward their final
reconciliation?

Did this have something to do with the metaphysical motivation
behind Joseph's hidden burial?

Do such traditions inform Mar Yusuf's ancient hope that not
only earthly divisions could be overcome by way of the "power of
repentance," but also heavenly ones, even between the forces of
good and evil themselves? That the death of the messiah created a
door, a way through which the universe could renew itself — no,
reconstitute itself — in repentance?

At the moment, I don't know how to make all of this clearer.
But there seems to be a river of Josephite connections whose
headwaters are to be found in this prayer. What am I asking,
really? Maybe I'm suspecting — as you've more than once implied,
Abba — that there really is a "gospel of Joseph," that is, not just

isolated religious themes drawn from a life (or traditions about that life), but an ideology — no, more, a *program*.

I am groping here, Abba Pachom. I have no convictions to defend, I can assure you, only questions....

[*Note:* The remainder of the text is missing.]

"Last Thoughts on Hidden Graves"
Two marginalia from the *Passion of Joseph the Just*

Unfinished typewritten note by Constantine Gruber; undated.

[*Note:* This note is the last entry by Gruber in the Joseph Archive. It was clearly intended as a first draft of a larger essay on two marginal jottings Gruber had deciphered in the *Passion* document. One suspects that the note was written at the very end of Gruber's involvement with the project, thus, shortly before his disappearance in the fall of 1951. —Ed.]

Marginal note from Leaf 16 of the *Passion*

In the Faiyumic dialect.

[*Note:* This short epigram provides us with our clearest evidence that, on the issue of Joseph's grave, the Mar Yusuf brotherhood firmly believed that the site was unknown. And not only that. For them, it was unknowable. —CG]

A fellah [peasant] asked a brother [monk] where the holy ones of Mar Yusuf were buried since he wished to honor the resting place of a deceased monk who had once given him good advice. But the brother laughed, and, kneeling down, placed his hand on the bosom of the earth: 'Should you wish to honor [the dead], you may do so here as well as anywhere.' For the 'sons of Joseph' [Mar Yusuf monks] are forbidden to mark their graves on account of their father [Joseph], whose grave is hidden in the heart of the world — that is, unknown. That is why the monks of Mar Yusuf never erect pillars or mark their graves with stones: It is so that they, too, may disappear into the heart of the world."

[*Note:* On the right margin of leaf 16 we find another marginal jotting on the same subject — the "hiddenness" of Joseph, and, by extension, one infers, the Josephite vocation. It is a late creation, however. Linguistic features allow us to assign it no earlier date than the seventeenth century. It reads like a folksong and, hence, one is not too surprised to find a version of it recorded in Arberry's useful *Folksongs of Middle Egypt* (Oxford, 1915). The lyric (actually a refrain, part of a larger poem), called "The Four Journeys," can still be heard when Copts from Assiyut province gather at Deir el-Muharrak on the Feast of the Assumption.

> "The builder, the builder had four journeys, four journeys:
> One for life to Bethlehem,
> Graceful as the geese on [Lake] Moeris,
> One for fear of kings [Herod] to Egypt,
> Swift as the eagle, swift as the eagle,
> One for the love of God to The Holy [Jerusalem],
> Mournful as the dove, as the dove,
> And one to die in the hidden place."

—CG]

Note from Constantine Gruber to Tamara Konen

Yellow legal pad, folded twice, clipped to a rag-paper Religion and Atheism Committee envelope.

October 8, 1951

Marra:

I'm leaving this note as we did in the old days in the custodian's closet rather than on the more intimate venue of my kitchen table. It's just that I won't be needing your help for the next few weeks. In view of your odd unavailability this past month, I trust that won't be too big a disappointment. You old friend Joseph, whom you have rather neglected of late, is slowly dematerializing. Soon the "Elijah chair" will be empty again, waiting for amiable Passover ghosts rather than the earthy redeemers we have had unsettling us these past months. It's all for the best, isn't it, Marra? The transcriptions are almost finished and the committee has managed to nearly starve me into submission over the "big thirty-three."[12] By the way, do you know of any particular reason why Hilda and the others would look particularly flustered whenever I mention your name? They do, you know.

GRUBER

Copy of telegram sent to Abba Pambon, care of general delivery, Alexandria

Still in its blue envelope quite apart from the Joseph Archive materials themselves; found by a university researcher stuffed in the leather pocket of the last notebook of the "Passion of Joseph the Just."

October 10, 1951
Leipzig, 9:30 A.M.

Father [stop] ordered cease all communications with Menas [stop] intend disobey [stop] consequences unknown [stop] joseph is safe.

[intercept: Niebel; cc to Konen]

[handwritten (a man's hand) in the right-hand margin: "Find him."]

With the text of this telegram, we come to the end of the documents currently at our disposal. The story ends as it began, half-lit, a tale of uncertainties: about the fate of Gruber, to be sure; but about the nature of the pages he translated as well. Luckily, it is not up to editors to find where the bodies are buried.

—THE EDITOR, *University of Leipzig Review*
May 29, 1989

12. The reconstruction of Maxim 33. —Ed.

Editor's Afterword:
The Last Monk of Mar Yusuf

Children occasionally manage to resist the projections of parents and the fateful decrees they promulgate over mangers. That, as the reader is undoubtedly aware, has proved the case with this "strange story" — it is the Builder's phrase — designated by its publishers for the ash-heap of academic monographs, only to make a name for itself virtually everywhere else but there in academia. Poor Schleyer, it would appear, is still in the dock before that bar with the ghosts of four age-black codices under his arm.

Since the publication of *The Gospel of Joseph,* however, further details have come to light about the circumstances of its latest (dare we say last?) incarnation in the form of Constantine von Gruber's translations.

That came about because of the archaeological frenzy that has overtaken post-communist Europe. In Yugoslavia, they are exhuming their war dead, and we in the new Germany are rustling the files of the former secret police with, one suspects, the same unsettling results. Having listened to a great deal of what the dead have to say, one must conclude, sadly, that they do not appear to be very respectful of the desires of the living. So much for ancestor worship in the 1990s.

Like others, the editors of the *Leipzig Review* hoped that the STASI (East German State Security Service) files would illuminate the many dark corners that haunt the Joseph Archive. And in that hope, we were not altogether disappointed. On the morning of April 15, 1991, three staffers came upon a single file folder in an annex of the former State Security Service in the former East Berlin on a shelf marked "DISPOSE"; it read: "The Gospel of Joseph Project: 1949–1951, State Committee on Religion and Atheism, 'Closed.' "

The file inventory sheet affixed to the large legal-sized folder listed twenty-three documents as having once comprised the dossier. Only two remained for us to examine, however: a yellowing memo addressed to Project Coordinator Martin Niebel, dated August 16, 1962, and an overwritten travel article published that same year in the Leipzig student paper *Morgen.*

While the STASI papers answer none of the fundamental questions that vex the case of the Joseph Archive, they do appear to settle, more or less, the essential questions surrounding Gruber's disappearance.

Given the range of echoes to which the Joseph documents give rise, it is not perhaps inconsequential that we can finally give at least one of them a decent burial.

—THE EDITOR, *University of Leipzig Review*

Contents of STASI file #332459(f)-Dept. R, sec. B-4

Document #1

Memorandum

To: Martin Niebel
        Chief of External Relations
        State Committee on Religion and Atheism

From: Tamara Konen
        Journalist

Re: Death of Constantine von Gruber

Date: August 16, 1962

Yes, Martin, all the information you had received from Khaled al-Buwayti, your agent at Al-Azhar [University in Cairo],[13] is correct: Constantine died five years ago in the Fayoum, near the village of El-Bustani, to be exact, some thirty miles southwest of the provincial town of Itsa.

Yes, I'm sure you know the place. It's where you suspected he had gone. It was nice of you, Martin, not to disturb him. But, then, you are not a bad man, you know; just a bureaucrat.

Cause of death: unknown. Even Khaled, who, as you know, has an opinion on virtually every subject known to man, could only hazard a guess. There had been an outbreak of typhus in the towns near the Joseph Canal [Bahr Yusuf] in the mid-fifties, so perhaps that had something to do with it.

As to the whereabouts of the codices, that's anybody's guess. Khaled thinks the monks of St. Menas have them. (They, of

---

13. Editor's insertions in brackets.

course, deny that.) But I have other ideas. It wouldn't surprise me to learn that they are with Constantine himself, that he had them buried with him. A venerable practice, no? The ancient Egyptians did it. And Constantine, he was a romantic fool, wasn't he, a figure from another age? Still, who would have thought him capable of all this?

No doubt, on learning your little secret, Martin, he feared for the fate of the manuscripts in the committee's careless hands. What would you have done with them, I wonder? Sold them on the black market when the cash flow from Moscow waned, had their large elegant leaves made into lampshades to provide interior decorating ideas for Party wives?

Did you ever really get a look at the originals, Martin? I first saw them in Constantine's flat, spread out on the kitchen table. What a still life that scene would have made: huge eternity-haunted volumes, big as a child, opened like epiphanies, and framed by the refuse of a far more disposable civilization — ash trays full of cigarette butts commingled with empty beer bottles.

Hardly a dialogue of equals, that much I can tell you.

The way the text lay on the page of the codices — it was a sanctuary for the play of dancing gods. Like the writing of children who leave great white spaces around their illuminations.

Not like us, chief, eh, who know better than to worship words? We prefer our language straight, lightweight, disposable, drained of blood. We chew on the bones.

But I digress.

Why did Constantine take the codices with him to Egypt? Well, my dear, it was a bit disorienting to discover as the translator of the Joseph Archive did in late 1951 that the State Committee on Religion and Atheism hadn't the slightest interest in the documents — and, what's more, never had. That's true, isn't it?

By the way, you must tell me sometime precisely how Gruber found out. Don't bother. It was undoubtedly Toppler, who is about as subtle as a fuse. I assume it was when he had managed a solution to the garbled thirty-third maxim of Joseph. I saw some of Constantine's cryptograms, you know, the puzzles he constructed to enable him to supply the missing text.

He had begun to suspect something because you all were driving him so hard to translate that single sentence, as if the whole future of the project depended on it. (Which, of course, it did.)

Toppler, for one, was a boor, ordering him to stay up night after night until he had puzzled it out, threatening to hold up his food rations until a translation was forthcoming. Who wouldn't start thinking that there had to be some other agenda at work, some purpose other than the mere translation of ancient documents behind the committee's enthusiasms?

And, as you know, Gruber succeeded. He did reconstruct the text on the basis of probabilities. (Did you even bother to see the result, Martin?) For the sake of the record, the lost Josephite maxim turned out to be not so much a saying as some kind of instruction or command to the "Nazarenes." Gruber thought the term referred (or so he told me) to the family of Christ:

> "THROUGHOUT THE AGES, THE NAZARENES SPEAK
> ONLY AS UNDERGROUND RIVERS [SPEAK]."

That was Gruber's guess, his reconstruction of the last maxim of Joseph. He told me then that he didn't know what it meant. But by then, perhaps, he had begun to have his doubts about all of us.

How could you gentlemen have entertained the idea that a conscientious Coptologist like Gruber would really go along with your scheme to send him to Moscow? And why the elaborate ruse? Wouldn't it have been easier to simply offer him the job as Kremlin cryptanalyst without the smokescreen of Schleyer's texts? I'm sure you had your reasons. Khaled shed a ray of light on the affair recently when he informed me that expertise in Coptic is considered a great advantage in cryptography, in the work of deciphering secret codes.

"Between the British and the Russians," he laughed, "it's very difficult to hold onto our Coptic scholars here in Egypt. They're always accepting these mysterious 'security' assignments in world capitals."

From the Builder to code-breaking: It was a stretch, you know.

So, I suppose, that means that the translation project served, in effect, as a kind of doctoral examination of Gruber's abilities. What a delicious irony, then, that the "test" maxim proved to be in Aramaic, not Coptic.

Well, well. I would have loved to have been there when he found out, Martin, but, as you know, I was already on to performing other tasks for the committee by then.

Still, I can't help but think there was something more to Gruber's flight with the goods than meets the eye. You must have thought so too. Otherwise, chief (may I suggest), you would have sent someone after him. I know, you were fond of him. He had — old Constantine — learned to speak our "language," the tongue of the empire of shadows, but, luckily for him, he never managed to become a citizen. And, I suppose, it deserves to be pointed out that having a large, costly debacle against Toppler on the casebooks proved not to be a bad thing for your career in the long run.

You remember that business about the monks of Mar Yusuf giving Schleyer the documents with the proviso that, upon request, they would be returned to the monastery? I know, Martin, details, details. But I think, in his heart of hearts, that's what Constantine was really up to: fulfilling the terms of the contract. In any case, he knew that the Joseph Archive was no longer safe in our Europe. The "Bedouin raiders" scavenging the countryside for "barterable treasures" — the original threat to the documents a century ago — they wear gray suits these days and speak a passable Russian.

Did we locate a grave? You quizzed me on that on the telephone from Cairo. Khaled asked around the village [El-Bustani], but all the locals would say is that the "German" — that's what they called him — wasn't interred in his monastic cell (that would be the normal Coptic practice for a solitary). In any case, according to all the information we have, Gruber was virtually the only actual full-time resident of Mar Yusuf, or what remains of it.

What must it have been like for old Gruber, one wonders, living in that ruin? From the looks of things, it must have been considerably less than a Byronic dream. Muslim villagers have long since commandeered the place. Rather more like camping out in a tenement house, I would think. And the youngsters pelted him with rocks at first, the locals said. That changed, however, when medicines and supplies began coming their way as a result of his frequent trips to Alexandria.

People were decidedly apprehensive when we began asking questions about Mar Yusuf. But when the nature of our business was made clear to them, they couldn't have been more cooperative. And when Khaled told them he was a communist, well, they were positively thrilled. You see, Martin, the villagers were not slow to find uses for the old place. Tobacco leaves festoon the arches of the cloister and the paving stones of the courtyard have been pulled up to make way for vegetable gardens of onions and radishes. Women wash their clothing in the ancient springs and farm animals inhabit the churches of St. Joseph and the Holy Virgin. There's even a tractor repair shop set up in the old guard house — that is, in what's left of the tower. Much of the stonework that once guarded a world of prayer today is found (shall we say) elsewhere.

The villagers are understandably wary about publication of the current uses to which they have put the monastery. Obviously, they have no legal right to commandeer the compound and should Khaled have materialized into a provincial bureaucrat or, worse, a lawyer for the Coptic patriarchate, there would have been trouble.

But a communist: He'd be expected to show a little enthusiasm for their shy irreverence.

The villagers even brought Khaled to an old man, a Christian, cared for by one of the Muslim families — God alone knows how old he is — in hopes of getting a little information. The man, it seems, ran errands for Gruber. But we could get nothing out of him. He was hopelessly senile.

According to people in the area, Gruber was visited from time to time by a monk of St. Menas near Alexandria. He seems to have been the last one to see Gruber alive. But, Khaled reports, the monks of St. Menas, to a man, deny the story and claim never to have heard that a European lived at Mar Yusuf.

In any case, the locals say, you can never know where a monk of Mar Yusuf lay buried. Their graves are all unmarked and there is not so much as a cemetery to be seen anywhere, that is, except the Muslim one on the outskirts of the village. "The 'sufis' " — that's how the local people refer to the monks — "they do not die, you know," the village elder told us with a smile, "they disappear."

Which reminds me, Martin: Do you mind very much if I "disappear" for a while — you know, take a break from assignments for the time being? Hilda's not well and Ilse, for that matter, is not much better. I do have obligations in that quarter, my friend. A duty self-imposed as your wife once suggested? Perhaps. But we were "related" [in Christ] once — Hilda, Ilse, Edith, and I — and they have no one else in the world anymore — no one alive, that is.

MARRA

Contents of STASI file #332459(f)-Dept. R, sec. B-4

Document #2

Excerpt from a travel piece published in the October 7 [1962] issue of the Leipzig student daily *Morgen*

"The Fayoum: Egypt's Forgotten Heartland"
by Tamara Konen, Senior travel writer

[*Note:* Most of the article is missing. From the look of it, much of what remains was period-piece Marxist blather about the joys of hydroelectric dams and the mechanization of agriculture. But the following section is underlined in red ink. Although the precise intent of those who maintained this file cannot be determined, this passage, clearly, was the reason for the document's inclusion in the records of the State Committee on Atheism and Religion. —Ed.]

... The Bahr Yusuf, or Joseph Canal, rises at Darut, as the so-called Second Nile or "ka," shadow of the Nile, as Emil Ludwig's now-classic text on the great river tells us (*The Nile,* 1937). This canal, named for the biblical patriarch Joseph, follows the course of the river like a wayward arabesque for more than 150 miles. Locals tell many colorful legends about this "second Nile." According to Muslim lore, it is even credited with being the source of the region's name.

The legend is told that the Jewish patriarch Joseph, the Pharaoh's vizier, was given, in old age, one last engineering project with which to prove his mettle. He was ordered to drain a vast marshland in order to provide an inheritance for one of Pharaoh's daughters. With heavenly guidance, the aged patriarch had three canals dug in a mere seventy days, by which he not only succeeded in draining the land, but claiming from the desert a great oasis in Middle Egypt. So the story goes, when Pharaoh saw what Joseph had accomplished, he said to his ministers, "What old Joseph has done in seventy, you could not do in a thousand days." Hence, according to the Arabs, the oasis was thereafter named "the land of a thousand days" — El-Fayoum.

Across the Joseph Canal, over the low Lybian hills, one enters into a great depression more than a hundred feet below sea level, fed by three watercourses and webbed with innumerable irrigation trenches. Writers throughout the ages have commented on the disturbing counterpoint the great valley affords of green fertility on the one hand and the litter of abandoned temples and cities on the other. Ludwig — a little melodramatically — calls the contrast the lakeshore of Qurun affords "sinister."

If one travels further on the road to the town of Itsa in the direction of Lake Qurun, one happens upon settlements at the edge of the oasis that, more than fifteen hundred years ago, played host to one of Egypt's most important, and fateful, exports: monasticism. In fact, a particularly unusual relic of that age stands today in one of the smaller and less visited villages in that region: a now-abandoned fourth-century foundation called Mar Yusuf [St. Joseph] after the so-called adoptive father of Jesus of Nazareth.

The writer is not suggesting that the site is worth visiting. There is nothing there to see in the village of El-Bustani in the heart of the Fayoum. As for Mar Yusuf, it is a memory. For rare, brief periods, an underground river comes to the surface there. That, as far as this writer can determine, is the only notable thing that happens in that locale. And, as such watercourses do, the stream soon ceases bubbling up in local wells and returns again to its mysterious path. Our readers, surely, are practical people, interested in and engaged with the visible world, the world that can be known and tasted, the world that can be touched. Our readers are not interested in underground rivers. . . .